THE LAMENTATIONS OF ZENO

THE LAMENTATIONS
OF ZENO

ILIJA TROJANOW

Translated by Philip Boehm

VERSO

London • New York

The translation of this work was supported in part by a grant from the Goethe-Institut, which is funded by the German Ministry of Foreign Affairs, and by an award from the National Endowment for the Arts.

First published in English by Verso 2016
Translation © Philip Boehm 2016
First published as *EisTau*
© Carl Hanser Verlag 2011

1 3 5 7 9 10 8 6 4 2

Verso
UK: 6 Meard Street, London W1F 0EG
US: 20 Jay Street, Suite 1010, Brooklyn, NY 11201
versobooks.com

Verso is the imprint of New Left Books

ISBN-13: 978-1-78478-219-1
ISBN-13: 978-1-78478-222-1 (US EBK)
ISBN-13: 978-1-78478-221-4 (UK EBK)

British Library Cataloguing in Publication Data
A catalogue record for this book is available from the British Library

Library of Congress Cataloging-in-Publication Data
Names: Trojanow, Ilija, author. | Boehm, Philip, translator.
Title: The Lamentations of Zeno : a novel / by Ilija Trojanow ; translated by Philip Boehm.
Other titles: EisTau. English
Description: Brooklyn, NY : Verso, 2016.
Identifiers: LCCN 2015039884| ISBN 9781784782191 (hardback) | ISBN 9781784782221 (US e book) | ISBN 9781784782214 (UK e book)
Subjects: LCSH: Glaciologists—Fiction. | Glaciers—Fiction. | Political fiction. | BISAC: FICTION / Political.
Classification: LCC PT2682.R56 E4713 2016 | DDC 833/.92—dc23
LC record available at http://lccn.loc.gov/2015039884

Typeset in Electra by Hewer Text UK Ltd, Edinburgh
Printed in the US by Maple Press

At each slow ebb hope slowly dawns that it is dying.

— Samuel Beckett, *Company*

Translator's Note

With *The Lamentations of Zeno*, Ilija Trojanow charts new territory in prose as well as geography. Not a native speaker of German, he has adopted that language and adapted it to his own purposes, taking full advantage of its lexical fecundity, creating words at will, and of its suspended syntax, with which he unleashes whole currents of consciousness. Alternating painterly descriptions of the natural world with cacophonic passages composed of song snippets, adspeak and "breaking news," he contrasts the majestic stillness of the Antarctic with the clamor of human "civilization." And all of this is framed within a confessional log that allows the reader to reconstruct the emotional course of the troubled protagonist.

The sheer range of registers is impressive — and quite a challenge for the translator. The title itself is a case in point: A literal "Ice Thaw" not only lacks the "aura" of the original *EisTau*, it also fails to convey the layers of meaning lurking in the German. "Melting Ice" seemed a bit lackluster, while "Meltdown" was more appropriate for any number of TV movies. Instead we decided to focus on the narrator who is the soul of the novel.

My primary task in translating the book has been to recreate the voice of Zeno Hintermeier—his gruff demeanor, deprecating self-irony, bone-dry wit, and great erudition. To this end I have broken up single-sentence paragraphs and recast them with somewhat shorter sentences easier on Anglophone ears. Otherwise punctuation remains light, echoing the German, although quotation marks have been added to set off some speech. Songs cited in the shorter bricolage passages have been substituted with popular English lyrics from the same period, and elsewhere I have similarly opted for equivalence over literal rendering.

Most of all I hope to have captured the deeper musicality of the prose, by paying as much attention to the rests as to the notes. Because for all his linguistic virtuosity Trojanow is equally a master of the unsaid, so that the words on the page are like the icebergs themselves—a sparkling intimation of what lies below.

THE LAMENTATIONS OF

1.

54°49′1″S, 68°19′5″W

THERE'S NO WORSE nightmare than no longer being able to save yourself by waking up.

Whenever we set sail from Ushuaia, we gather the evening before in one of the local dives that's a little ways uphill and off the main streets, just when the last band of light is slipping from the sky. We haven't seen one another for half a year, so we're in the mood to celebrate as we crowd around a long wooden table. The man waiting on us is old, and judging by his face not very adventurous, although at one parting he confessed to me that he was getting along well apart from an occasional urge to puncture his hand with a knife. His place doesn't have much on offer, but he'll fill your glass for very little and I'm content to sit here holding my drink, surrounded by the hardworking Filipinos that make up most of the crew, now smiling broadly at our reunion. Every payday brings them closer to settling down to a home and the sheltering shade of a large family, and so they soldier on, slogging through their working days with an astounding ease. For me they will always be an enigma. Ushuaia is incapable of dampening their mood, as is any echo of the butchery, any painful reminder of the past—their ears are simply not tuned to that frequency, that legacy belongs to Europeans, those are the scars of the white man. They drift through this place just as they do through all the other places that have been defiled, all our ports of call (what a pretentious phrase from some liturgy of advertising), seeming not to touch the ground when they go ashore. That is what separates us, we have no common past: what paralyzes me seems to fill them with life. Apart from that, they're "easy to handle," as our onboard hotel manager never tires of repeating (by which he means: much better than the unruly Chinese), as if he had personally trained them to be so diligent so patient so tame. The Filipinos' zeal would bother me were it not for Paulina, who at this moment is probably busy giving a personal touch to our shared cabin, equipping it with artificial flowers and photographs depicting an entire menagerie of relatives—the numerous grandmothers perched in front on dilapidated rattan armchairs dragged into the garden just for the occasion, and standing behind them all the daughters and sons, loyal to a man except for the one who ran off and is rumored to be chopping vegetables in a New York restaurant. I raise my glass to Paulina's countrymen—mechanics, cooks, pilots—and to Ricardo, our dining room manager, as unobtrusive as a

shrink-wrapped suitcase, but watch out, his true power
will be revealed during the course of the trip, every passenger will get to know him and a few will appreciate him
("Howzit going, Mr. Iceberger?" he says, giving me a
thumbs-up, always concerned to clear potential misun-
derstandings out of the way before they happen). It's a
sight for the gods, the way the millionaires from the northern hemisphere line up in front of his desk, eagerly bowing
as they slip him an envelope to thank him for the coveted
starboard table with a box-seat view of ice floes and leopard seals. My recent years at sea have taught me that rich
people are prepared to pay considerable sums for little
privileges. That sets them apart from the masses, feeds
Ricardo's confidence, and finances the expansion of his
guesthouse in Romblon. He's no more interested in fur
seals, leopard seals or penguins than he is in glaciers or
icebergs, but he takes advantage of every scenic opportunity—"What a view, fantastic, fantastic, please take your
seats,"—as he parades his teeth in a broad grin. I'm sure
he'd squeeze in just as many "fantastics" in front of a
garbage depot as long as there were people willing to pay
for a premium seat. All he really cares about is whether
something is sellable or not. Whenever we're all together
he flirts with the blonde whale lady now sitting to his left,
always resorting to the same lines, which he polishes like
a fingernail, "You know some day I'm going to sit in on
your lecture, I mean it, I really want to learn all about
these fish, now that I've watched them from the restaurant and seen them spouting, they really are very beautiful creatures"—but when it comes to the beautiful Beate

he has a hard time understanding why she prefers whales to people, which is why he's going to sit in the first row during one of her next lectures and write down every single word she says. He promises this before every trip, when we're gathered at the long wooden table that's pitted and scored with random dents and notches. "This time I mean it," he says, "I swear to heaven"—and the whale lady pinches his arm. She speaks English with a German accent, German with a hint of Spanish, and Spanish with Chilean intonation. Despite his assurances, nothing will come of Ricardo's "cetacean education." But what he will do for certain at the end of the trip is pass a chef's hat around on behalf of the men in the kitchen, while they line up in front of the curved buffet and perform a song in Tagalog that sounds like the "Hymn to the Unknown Server" and is always received with thunderous applause.

The experts aboard the MS *Hansen* are also at the table, the lecturers tasked with educating the vacationers, just like I was doing for three years until yesterday when the captain summoned me just after my arrival and told me the expedition leader had been taken unexpectedly to the hospital in Buenos Aires with a suspected case of swine flu, there was no way he'd be able to join us at this point, at best we might be able to pick him up along the way, further down the Beagle Channel, but until then a substitute is needed, and he believes I have the necessary competence, I know the subject, I'm engaged, and I am worldly-wise (here his glance implied I also might be inclined to overshoot my target on occasion), and apart from that I have a lot of experience on board the ship. I neither wanted to agree with his assessment nor decline the offer, so I took the folder with the instructions. From now on I'll be spending far too much time using the radio and the PA system, keeping the passengers up to date on the weather, the route, our next destination. Each of the lecturers has a special field of expertise—oceanography biology climatology geology—and each of us knows how to talk about animals clouds cliffs both instructively and entertainingly. And each of us is a refugee in his own weird way: in the words of El Albatros, our Uruguayan ornithologist, "We're really just a bunch of nowhere people." He nods my way, "Mr. Iceberger"—he calls me that too, some of them have never used my real name, Zeno, and others aren't sure how to pronounce it, whether Zen-know or Zee-no or Say-no (this from the mouth of our whiz kid Jeremy from California, who could practically be my grandson). These are minor matters to which I attach no importance, but I have the sneaking suspicion my colleagues use the nickname to disguise their belief that I'm some kind of misfit or freak. And it is more than a bit bizarre to be considered too passionate by people so passionately dedicated to their own pursuits.

Earlier that day Beate escorted a group of passengers to the national park, where paths wind along the coves and the sun's rays angle down and settle on individual leaves like butterflies. We've all taken this easy walk through the virgin Patagonian forest at one time or another, but this year they've opened a new path and the ever-conscientious Beate has no intention of letting some tourist embarrass her by knowing more than she does, even if it's just about a few new dots on a map and a path to a further cove. For that reason, as she explains at length, she took a bus past the southernmost golf course in the world, past the end of Pan-American Highway, to a wide, leveled parking lot where people land in the middle of nature like so many aliens, and where a small stairway of freshly treated wood leads up to the path.

"How many whales did you spot?" Ricardo asks jokingly.

"One," says Beate.

"Just one whale, how is that possible? A loner? A juvenile?"

"A beached whale very much on land and made of stone with moss on top. A whale that children are allowed to ride on." Beate pauses. "It's sitting out there like a memento mori." She pauses even longer. "The thing looks massive enough that it might actually stand the test of time, too. The new path has trashcans every two hundred meters and benches every two hundred meters: trashcan bench trashcan bench as you go stalking through the forest. Our guide was a creep in tall boots, a Buenos Aires *porteño* who likes the notion of spending his summer in the fresh air of the south, he spoke in a high falsetto voice as if to balance out his very low level of knowledge, he talked about the original inhabitants as though they were wild animals, didn't even mention their name, 'grass-chewers' is what he called them, and he made stupid jokes like 'we don't know much about them, they were so shy, the minute they caught sight of a person they turned tail and scrammed and if you tried to approach them they hid deep in the bush like hedgehogs or burrowed underground like skunks.' I couldn't help myself, I had to teach him a lesson in front of the passengers: the people who once lived in this forest were called *Yah-gan*. He repeated the word as if he had to crack it open, '*Yah-gan*— well that fits a primitive natural tribe just about as well as a fist fits an eye, it sounds foreign, like some strange species of spider.' Did I mention his boots? They left deep prints, and some name or other, probably that of the manufacturer, got stamped into the earth with every step he took. Primitive natural tribe, can one of you tell me where a phrase like that comes from?" Beate stops speaking, and a hush falls over the table as though by some prearranged signal. Not everyone heard the question, but the answer will spread across the entire table.

"Because we wiped them out," I say in a loud voice. "Because we destroy everything aligned with nature. We honor the people who are extinct, we put their masks on display and print their portraits in sepia, we show enormous care and devotion to those we have exterminated."

The lecturers all start to sigh—here he goes again, they're all expecting one of my diatribes, I've subjected them to an avalanche of rage on more than one occasion. They know from experience that whenever Mr. Iceberger waxes apodictic things will end apocalyptic. But it's our first shared evening, so I bite my tongue and say nothing more as other conversations begin to rustle around the table.

All the others leave but me, I stay behind with the old man who spent the whole evening waiting on us in silence. That's become a custom with the two of us, since the first time I sought him out. I had left my

camera on one of the wooden benches in his bar and
walked back through the cold. It was very windy and I
was nearly frozen when I went inside, the old man was
cleaning up, all by himself, he had to fix something to
get me warm and on top of that grant me a conversation, which at first made us feel even more like strangers, but then sentence by sentence, shot by shot, we let
down our armor to the point of showing our wounds.
Since then we've never been far from each other in our
thoughts. He quietly wipes down the table with circular
motions, the veins on his hand look like glacial stria-
tions, his skin shows a number of liver-brown patches.
With implacable anger he curses his fate to be born,
grow up and grow old here in Ushuaia, which has always
been a makeshift place, where every shop is called
Finisterre and every apron is plastered with penguins, to
live in this spot that shows no pity for anyone, not for
those who once roamed barefoot over thorns until they
were killed by adventurers seeking their fortune or by
civil servants fallen into disfavor, not for those banned
to the penal colony in heavy chains, whose yearning to
escape cut deeper and deeper into their flesh and not
for their descendants who grovel before the tourists as if
they wanted to pick the dried bits of mud off their boots,
as if the earth of Tierra del Fuego still contained gold
dust. Does a place change for the better when people
move away of their own accord? Does peat that has been
drenched in blood still spread warmth when it burns on
a homey hearth? The old man disappears for a moment
and returns with two bulbous snifters of a drink that

smells like vanilla and leaves a nice burn in the throat.
The old man doesn't stop moving, from the counter to
the tables, from one table to the next, as if something
needed to be tied down in every spot. I follow him to
the window, the sparsely set streetlamps blur in the driz-
zle into muted trickles of light. We stand for a moment
listening to the distant sounds. Suddenly he resumes
speaking.

"As a child I used to spend the afternoons hanging
around in front of our house—this place used to be our
shack—and I'd gaze down at the town. Sometimes, when
the sky was so overcast the clouds seemed to touch the
ground I had the feeling the street might vanish with the
fog. I'd race down the street full of expectation but every
time I just landed in the filth of the harbor."

Finally we sit down, and he refills our glasses as if there
were plenty in stock. Long sentences of silence are punc-
tuated by his pronouncements:

"Whoever tries to live an honest life in this place is
punished with a shot in the back of the neck."

"We paid homage to my murdered grandfather in fear-
ful silence."

"My mother warned me about men in uniform the way
other mothers warn their children about mean alley cats."

Suddenly he turns to me, looks me in the eye and says,

"You're setting off again and once again you're letting
everything happen. You're defiling your own temple."

He rubs his hand across his face, his beard.

"I've been watching you. You're nothing but talk. Your
indignation is a fart. You let off steam, you shoot your

mouth, but otherwise you're just like all the others, no, you're worse, because you understand, and you sell your knowledge for a few pieces of silver."

I don't contradict him, and that makes him even more furious.

"Anyone who just accepts what can be avoided is a scoundrel." He's practically screaming. And then he shows me the heavy door.

As if I were half made of moraine, that's the nightmare I have every night.

Tomorrow the passengers come on board. Day one: embarkation. A day like any other. We have yet to set sail. The impending departure makes me uneasy, I wasn't born a sailor, on the contrary, my home was the mountains, before I was chased away. The first time I saw the ocean was at the mouth of a glacier, the glacial tongue was practically licking the beach, the glacial stream was running ahead of me, I was in my early twenties and confident, so confident I purposely got lost in the rainforest between the beach and the glacier. Today that glacier has melted away and its phantom tongue visits me in my sleep to mock me and I am powerless against my nightmare's minions. Paulina is already slumbering away, she falls asleep quickly, more quickly if we've made love. Tomorrow we set out. One more tour. My fourth year.

It is written.

We let ourselves be comforted by demeaning sentences such as this. Nothing is written: it is being written. By every single one of us. Just like everyone contributes his little bit to all the poisoned ruins on this earth. Hence this notebook, hence my decision to describe what has happened, what will happen. I shall be the word-keeper of my own conscience. Something has to happen. There's no time to waste.

··· — — — ···

Measurements to die for check her out I tell you, nobody gives a hoot, you can kiss it goodbye, grab yours now while supplies last. Sir, we're picking up a distress signal on 406 MHz. Screw up your courage, measurements to die for, you'll be licking your lips afterward, thirteen months of sunshine, welcome to paradise, and it rained every single day. Distress beacon? Yes sir. Which ship? It isn't clear, sir. The chapel's been closed for a week now, the frescoes are being renovated, no it won't open again until the fall, I'm sorry you've come all this way in vain, we can't allow ourselves to be pressured, a question for your guest, all you have to do is switch a few letters and contribution becomes retribution, something's stuck, something always gets stuck. I have a fix, sir at 43°22' S and 64°33' W. All ravens are black, I've had it up to here, the apparent temperature was higher, measurements to die for, she'll make better speed on the lee side, cut to the chase, it's a done deal. Something isn't right, sir, we've lost radio contact with the *Hansen*. What about their radio officer? He's not responding, sir. Hey hey hey get your fingers off it's my turn, the bra's all mine, ok Charlie hold your breath, ready one two and come on damn hooks got snagged, there'll be better days to come. Radar? Moving north-northwest. You've tried all channels? Yes, sir. Keep trying, I'm calling the Argentine coast guard. I'd like to ask your guest a question, if I understand correctly we're all either going to heaven or else to hell, but one way or other we're all going somewhere, so does that mean we're essentially immortal? Prefectura Naval Argentina? Sí . . . sí . . . Her last position given was 54°49' S 68°19' W, no we haven't had any contact with the *Hansen* since then. No doubt about it, they're going to shoot that bird down, don't take it so to heart, go ahead and catch your breath, take a deep breath, measurements to die for, we're doing what we can, and there is something we can do BREAKING   NEWS   ACCIDENT   IN   THE ANTARCTIC?   BREAKING   NEWS   ACCIDENT   IN THE   ANTARCTIC? and nevertheless

••• − − •••

2.

55°05′0″S, 66°39′5″W

BEFORE WE PUT out to sea, all passengers must prove they are healthy (not in perfect health, just healthy enough). They make their way upstairs or downstairs to Deck 4— those with medical restrictions use the elevator—and line up in front of the dapper Brazilian doctor with his vaunted head of curls. The man looks incredibly taut and trim in his uniform, the result of spending every free minute in the coffin-sized fitness room, listening to heavy metal from São Paulo, his eyes fixed on the emergency exit. I've never been able to talk to him. All those declared fit proudly brandish their medical clearance like a coveted concert ticket, they introduce themselves, exchange ideas, they've been to this place and that, well we're generally up for anything, but the heat, and what about the insurgents, on the other hand, there are so many places we'd like to see it's impossible to choose where to go next, of course first we have to survive this little adventure. For present purposes everyone is healthy enough, though they might be mere heartbeats away from a coronary or a stroke.

We set sail at last light. Our leave-taking is perfunctory: no one waves goodbye, not from the deck and not from the dock. Virtually no one is staying behind in Ushuaia, at least no one we'll miss. I enjoy standing on the topmost deck, musing over the silhouettes. I loathe sunsets because they reduce such a wealth of possibilities to a single effect. No one tries to engage me in conversation, the guests don't know me yet, neither the lecturers nor the expedition leader will be introduced until tomorrow after breakfast. We cast off without fanfare and are heading east through the Beagle Channel at approximately seven knots, according to my estimation, which after a few seasons on board is fairly accurate. Take a look at that cliff, a passenger calls out, like a giant with a sixpack. The group pounds its laughter into the twilight. And once again out come the camcorders and once again nature is diminished in the zoom of their lenses. I retreat to the port side.

"Hey there! Don't run away!" The pianist is heading straight toward me, in his wake a visage emerges from the darkness, and beneath the festive lights I am able to make out a less-than-shipshape face. "Allow me to introduce you. Mrs. Morgenthau, this is our new expedition leader, a perfect model of a gentleman"—the pianist is British—"I'm certain he can answer your question satisfactorily, our expedition leader can provide a satisfactory answer to any question." Our pianist passes for a great wit.

"That's kind of you, very kind, as a matter of fact I was just asking about that mountain, it's so dramatic the way it simply rises up there, surely it has a name?"

"Mount Misery." My answer is geographically correct, but the American's disbelieving look is virtually an accusation. The pianist grins at his well-played practical joke.

"Please, Madam, don't be shy about asking the expedition leader whatever you fancy in the course of our passage, whenever you feel the need. As for the evening concert I myself am happy to take requests, otherwise I just plunk along, as I'm sure you'll hear."

"The people who used to live in this region," I continue, "were aquatic nomads, they had many names for the mountains, the rivers, the forest. They developed a rich vocabulary for describing what surrounded them without wanting to possess it. Their name for this strait was something like 'the water that stabs through the twilight.'"

"And the island we just passed, you know the one I mean, I'm sure it has a magnificent name as well?" the pianist asks. He knows the answer but I do him the favor and play along.

"It's called Fury Island."

Another mistrustful look.

"Yes, of course, Fury Island, and here I'd done such a nice job of suppressing that one. Come, my dear, let's not trouble our expedition leader any longer, incidentally I ought to warn you now so you don't find out from some unreliable source that sometime in the middle of the night, when I trust we'll all be sound asleep, our ship is going to sail past Last Hope Bay."

His laughter rises and floats away like steam from an exhaust pipe.

That first evening Paulina's shift ends before midnight. The guests haven't had any time to get to know one another, the habitual drinkers and loungers quit the bar and bistro earlier than usual, Paulina hastens the last call and ushers an elderly American to his bed, she's looking forward to our more spacious cabin (befitting the post of expedition leader), and to me as well, we haven't yet had a chance to celebrate our reunion. I've been promoted to Deck 6, where the commanding elite is housed, my cabin is next door to the first officer and the chief navigator, and not far from the bridge, in fact a little earlier I stepped into the passageway and ran smack into the captain, whose office and refuge are just a few doors down and across the hall.

"Our captain's literally within striking distance," I tell Paulina.

"Well don't hurt him," she laughs. And I laugh back. I'm always amazed at how easily we make each other laugh, time and time again. I used to be thought a killjoy, and with good reason: what others considered hilarious I found obnoxious, I would hear them snicker and cluck, but never really laugh, my former spouse used to giggle and cackle her way through an evening, she could be loud and brash, but there was no real exuberance, no jollity. Paulina on the other hand gets me to laugh as she's taking off my clothes, stripping me down to a pure good mood. For her, laughter and libido are very much intertwined.

When our bodies have been so long apart, rediscovery follows conquest, and in between forays she lies next to me, feet crossed, her vulva gently vaulted, and chatters away as I listen to her lapping voice. It's the most calming human sound I know. So much has happened in the months we've been apart, a waterfall of events, the Mayon volcano erupting, the neighbors' child and his cleft lip surgery, the massacre of more than two dozen journalists on the next island over, the old fisherman whose right hand was blown off, her mother's worsening blindness, her brother's increasing dull-mindedness, her sister's infertility, the lecherous priest caught red-handed in the presbytery just after mass, his cassock tossed over the back of the receptive widow, and the rest of the story is drowned in laughter. But what should I tell her? About my weekly visits to my father and how he spews at anyone who takes pains to deal with him: the nurse, the doctor, the cook, his acquaintances from home (he hasn't had any friends since the end of the last war) — even the taxi driver who takes him to the cemetery three times a week so he can reassure himself that his place is still there next to my long-deceased mother, his "wee patch of earth" which he claims to look forward to. When I separated from my institute and my wife separated from me, I invited him to move in and take over Helene's gapingly empty bedroom. Now and then he'd wake me up at three in the morning with his yelling, and I'd get out of bed and see him shuffling across the hall holding a candle and shouting at every shadow cast by his shaky hand: "I'm a heretic too." It took a while for him to calm down, sometimes until morning, he never let on what accusation he was refuting. He's been considered a hardheaded heckler and contrarian his whole life, and the reputation has proved convenient. He banged on the table but never budged it. Roared but never bit. Now that his life force is trickling away, his vituperation has shriveled into a chronic dry cough. Should I burden Paulina by telling her my father has missed the right time to die? I'd rather take refuge in the stories she tells, they're much less pathetic than my own.

For months Paulina and I inhabit this ship together, sharing our cabin, and then we go our separate ways for half a year, losing sight of each other completely. It wouldn't even bother me to learn that during our time apart she'd gotten together with the Coca-Cola dealer from Legazpi City (the man never tires of fawning over her, though to date he hasn't offered anything better than an invitation to become his mistress). I feel about Paulina the way old Amundsen felt about the sun, I look forward to seeing her again but do not suffer terribly by her absence. On occasion we have tried to shorten the interval: after our first season in the eternal ice Paulina came to visit me, but it didn't go well. One neighbor congratulated me on my "catch" and another asked her if she'd clean for him, too. Paulina couldn't understand why I didn't own a car even though I could afford one, a deficiency that during the course of a very rainy April became increasingly conspicuous, my native country was only tolerable when viewed from the top of the Zugspitze (for the first time in my life I took the cable car, she wouldn't even try a descent), and so we slogged through the days, and our voices began to grate on each other while our desire passed faster than our time together. My own guest performance on Luzon had a number of sour notes as well, almost overnight she turned into an obedient little cog, was no longer Paulina but the eldest daughter, the wealthy sister, while I was a souvenir from a foreign land proudly put on display. But sooner or later the novelty wears off and the knickknack's merely in the way and winds up getting moved from one corner to the other until it's finally ignored completely. I didn't want to wait for that to happen, so I went to the market and hopped on a bus with the promising name Inland Trailways. I drove across the country, searching every face for a hint of Paulina but finding only strangers. When I flew home everyone at the airport was wearing mouth protectors, like so many idolatrous masks.

But as the northern summer draws to an end we reunite far in the south, happy and together. Here in the Antarctic we are made for each other, and Paulina is a blessing I had no right to expect.

"How was the ice mass balance last season?" a passenger who's traveled with us before asks the captain over our first dinner. "I've never seen so much pack ice at the start of a season," the captain replies, "and never seen so much green at the end of one."

••• — — •••

Sparrows chirp it from the roofs, we fled to the south where dollars drop from the sky like snowflakes, everyone must be called upon to sacrifice, place your order while supplies last, the museum is closed, water damage, the roof was old and decrepit, and now for the high point of our evening, I can't stand these fat-asses in their gas guzzlers, these turbo-charged jerk-offs in their Escalades. There's a problem with one of our ships, the MS *Hansen*, we've lost radio contact. Now it's your turn, Charlie, that belt really suits you, you go goldfingers, and a one and a two and a three unzip that mini watch it drop feel your balls about to pop, lights webcam action. I can affirm that the MS *Hansen* is on the wrong course, moving north-west at top speed, that's right we still don't have radio contact, we don't have any explanation, we'll have to be on standby for every possible emergency situation. Now that's what I call one efficient move, lol, our next contestants will face the fun task of making a meaningful sentence out of the words "folderol" and "poppycock," the first one to meet the challenge will receive our coveted Triple Twaddle Prize, we insist on having an international commission, that has to be examined very closely, in London unexplained delays held up today's fixed price for nickel, that's a great solution, all bad things come in threes and fours and twos. No, no mayday, no indication of any problems, no mention of disturbances in the daily report. I say let's cordon off the streets, and haul out every one of those turbo-charged jerk-offs and make them choose, your Cadillac or your cock, well underway, a little joke on the side, Christians view the desert as a place of evil, it's really the ultimate place of good, how could all your intuitions be so far off the mark your Grace, hey that's one shaved pussy, we're moving our webcumcam in for a better view, oom bop bop I'm pickin' up good vibrations, Charlie which of our legs are you trying to pull, what are you sniffing at, what I'm gonna pull is between those thighs, the difference between earthworms and chimpanzees, between punks and porters is purely a matter of cultural determinism, attention attention BREAKING NEWS NATURE NOT IN DANGER, PEOPLE FEARED DEAD BREAKING NEWS NATURE NOT IN DANGER, PEOPLE FEARED DEAD keep it up

•• • — — •••

3.

53°22´5˝ S, 61°02˝ W

FROM THE BEGINNING, it was the chance to talk about ice that inclined me to take the assignment, which fluttered into my home out of an overcast sky when my colleague Hölbl came to the door masquerading as a harbinger of good news. He closed his umbrella and asked if he should take off his shoes before entering. I can't remember whether he said, "I'm planning an attempt on your life" or "Can you do me a favor?" if he grinned at me or scrutinized me. At that point the institute was seething with rumors that I was going to pot without work without marriage without anything I could obsess about, I was notoriously easy to get worked up, have you noticed he's no longer accepting any invitations, but then he never was very sociable to begin with (I've always been suspicious of words that begin with the letters "S-O-C-I"—society is a mirage, sociable makes me think of chattering skulls, sociology is more a bog than a field), he's mutating into a complete recluse, he's on the verge of losing it, those are the rumors according to Hölbl, but in spite of his sarcastically upbeat report it was impossible not to hear a genuine note of concern in his voice and see the honest wrinkles of worry in his face—it all moved and angered me at the same time. When it comes to the countless people who grind away for wages that are less than inspiring, who get sores on their fingers and scabs in their brains, the Hölbls of this world never suspect mental or spiritual decline. From his viewpoint I was sick, an acute case of ice deprivation. But he was cunning and did not disclose the therapeutic motive for his visit on this rainy autumn day, instead he begged me to help him out of a mess he'd gotten himself into, he'd made conflicting commitments, accepted one thing without canceling the other, the usual polygamist trap (Hölbl was trying his best to cheer me up). He tempted me with everything he could, including the amorous adventures to be found on the high seas, which he touted so vividly as though I'd just been released from the convent boarding school, on a ship it was easier to catch a playmate than a cold, and I could enjoy things without any complications, because what happened at sea stayed at sea, my recuperation was guaranteed, there were no students (Hölbl was lowering himself somewhat with these efforts at humor), just a few lectures, some trips out to the penguin colonies, and that was basically it, all in all a lucrative form of sloth, "busy working holiday" is what they call it on board, you'll master the nautical language in two shakes, you know the subject matter in your sleep, your English is down pat, I have to pull out, meanwhile

take a look at the pictures I brought. Hölbl was too stingy
to print real photos, he'd run off some cheap copies on
regular paper, the color looked very artificial. I spread
them out on the coffee table, next to each other, on top of
each other, completely covering the wooden border. They
all seemed familiar—the snow-polished ice, the ribs and
furrows gleaming in the sun, the crystalline undulations—
and yet I was looking at an unknown world, where glaciers
calved into an ocean instead of a valley. Taken together,
the photos conjured some benevolent spell that had been
spun outside of time, every word that the Antarctic water
was whispering to me was frozen, I picked up one of the
photos as carefully as I could but still left a fingerprint on
one of the icebergs. "Pretty intense, isn't it?" Hölbl stood
beside me, with an almost lewd grin, "Damned intense is
what it is," he said, his laugh exploding like a firecracker as
he slapped his right hand on the back of the chair. There
are moments when you have no choice but to laugh along
whether you want to or not, if you don't want to lose your
common language. Weeks later I was standing on somewhat shaky legs in the auditorium of a cruise ship, amazed
at how many passengers showed up for my first lecture
(9:30 AM in English and 11 AM for the German version),
my biggest audience ever, what I had lost in terms of
younger listeners was more than compensated for by the
overdose of seniors. These passengers feel an obligation to
ground themselves, to learn what they can about the
Antarctic, they board the ship knowing little but truly
desire to learn more, that suits me just fine, by all means
permit me to influence your vision of the unknown. On

this trip which is unlike any other, they delve into the literature to further their education instead of devouring thrillers as they do elsewhere, for relaxation they prefer *The Worst Journey in the World*, such close encounters with the Eternal Ice causes even the civilizationally autistic to feel a certain lack within themselves. I hear myself talking and wonder at my chatty tone: when Africa slammed into Europe, Antarctica went skidding as far south as it could and got covered with ice, the crumple zone that resulted forms what we call the Alps. Antarctic means "anti-arctic," the name derived from Aristotle's postulation that for philosophical harmony and geographical symmetry there had to be a counterpart to the icy land in the north (the only such land then known to the Europeans). Anyone who claims never to have mixed up Arctic and Antarctic is a boldfaced liar, but there's a mnemonic device that can come to your aid, actually two devices, a bear and a penguin, since as we all know penguins are found only in the Antarctic and polar bears only in the Arctic regions. And this all makes sense because the word "arctic" comes from the ancient Greek *arktos*, having to do with Ursa Major—the big bear. So if you can just hold on to that you'll never mix up north and south again, in contrast to all of your friends at home, whose first question will be how things are going down there in the Arctic. Of course if polar bears become extinct, the name "Arctic" will no longer apply and we'll need something else, I'm happy to take suggestions beginning today and for the rest of our journey. But have no fear, even if the Arctic should cease to exist (something all of you sitting in this room will live to see if you keep taking your blood thinners and beta blockers—I don't speak this last thought out loud), the Antarctic will remain as an antipode for as long as humans inhabit the Earth. A few passengers smile, some smirk. Together we wander through the history of ice and stone with the help of a timetable where *Homo sapiens* barely appears, some days I have to really work to make sure the passengers don't faint from all the zeroes. Arctic and Antarctic, ladies and gentlemen, we are talking about extreme contrasts: seasonal ice in one place and terra firma in the other, unstoppable melting in one place, and in the other an icy shield up to four thousand meters deep. One place doomed to collapse, the other somewhat protected and not yet lost. One place a sign of our capacity for destruction, the other a symbol of our understanding. In a nutshell: above is bad, below is good, above is hell, below is heaven. Ladies and gentlemen, what we are talking about are the two poles of our future. Before opening the second PowerPoint presentation, I pause longer than necessary to let my ominous emphasis take effect before substantiating my claims with pictures, just like Hölbl did on my coffee table, but whether they're printed on cheap copy paper or displayed on a high-definition screen, the ice landscapes possess such force that the entire audience is rendered coughless, and together we plunge into the high-sea silence of the albatross.

Did Hölbl have any inkling what his visit would unleash? Anyone who only knows ice as a caged animal in closed valleys is bound to be overwhelmed by the radical freedom of the white south, where all exceptions are the rule, where ice covers everything except the steepest cliffs. Landscapes like this didn't exist even in the wildest dreams of the eight-year-old boy who together with the others from the same apartment block dared one another to drink water from a puddle with a straw, until some mother spotted them through one of the open windows and let loose a cry that landed right in the middle of their game.

"Come on up here boy," my father called out, without leaning out the window, "we're going to the mountains."

I went up immediately.

"Why the short britches?"

"It's hotter than blazes out there."

"You'll be cold."

"No I won't, Papa, believe me I won't get cold."

"Well we'll see about that . . ."

In my memory my father leaves Mittersendling in second gear and stops at every crossing. Our motor sounds happy and I'm bouncing on the seat so as not to miss anything. Father imitates different birds with chirps and twitters, he's a robin a greenfinch a woodpecker.

"You should be on the radio, Papa."

"With all that twitteratura, for an hour of bird calls? Nobody'd put up with it."

"No I mean mixed together with all the singers, they'd do a song, you'd do a bird . . ."

"How would that work? Ladies and gentlemen, stay tuned for The Blackbirds' latest hit? They wouldn't put up with it for even a second. Well, we'll see about that . . ."

I'm allowed to roll down the window, after that I can no longer hear the twittering. My father's had the VW Beetle for just a few weeks, before that he took the streetcar, and we used the sidewalk. Wherever we couldn't get on our own two feet we didn't belong. I count the oncoming cars as well as the ones overtaking us. Red cars count twice, I don't remember why. Right when I've reached a hundred points my father announces that we're almost there, the trip didn't take long, three hours, maybe three and a half. We park the car and hike up a path, and all at once I see a wall and feel a wave of cold that's unusual for the middle of summer. Driving back hours later, I rub my hands over the goose-pimples on my upper thigh, feel my wet shoes and stare at the disappearing vista, you'll get sick, Papa warns, but I refuse to let go, I'm staring at the glacier through two panes of glass, like looking at my future through a pair of binoculars, in the end I didn't let go. Everything's backward, I told my mother later, it's like a dragon with ice-cold breath instead of fire just lying there spitting out ice and spitting out ice and there's no stopping. You won't believe the ice that's up there, waterfalls that are frozen caves but they aren't really caves, they're chapels, they're all blue like your favorite dress, and so smooth. The minute you sit down you go sliding off on the seat of your pants. And Papa said that when somebody dies up there on the glacier his body gets swallowed and doesn't get spit out until his grandchildren go searching for him. Papa said the ice is full of frozen faces (as a student I used to proclaim with the arrogance of experts that no statue can come close to the ice sculptures, one day at the glacier is worth more than a hundred years in the Pinakothek). I told the other kids from the courtyard about my discovery, about my glacier, I told my schoolmates and all my cousins when we went to Wolfratshausen for my grandmother's birthday. I even told my grandfather. He was sitting by the corner shrine, his nostrils had little black crumbs like snot, he listened to me stock-still and finally said: "You're going to see a thing or two, lad." I went on and on, talking until I was blue in the face, now I hear myself talking once again, after a downward slide into silence, talking more than ever, since I'm being listened to, the passengers are sitting in their rows, the Antarctic is a repository for all of us, the ice contains air bubbles that have been trapped for thousands of years, as if the Earth regularly cleared its lungs, exhaling present moments that are caught and securely stored in these natural coffers, every volcanic eruption, every eclipse, every atomic weapon test, every shift in the concentration of atmospheric carbon dioxide (every fart of mankind is how Jeremy puts it when nobody's around). And don't forget, I tell them in closing, you're going to see a lot of ice on our trip, and you'll be shivering with cold, for some of you it will be the first time you've felt that kind of cold, and nevertheless what you will be seeing is all in the banana belt of Antarctica during the warmest part of summer. Think about it, there's hardly any region in the world warming up as quickly as the Antarctic peninsula, before long we'll see heather growing, and potatoes being planted, and sheep grazing, and after that it won't be much longer before people start vinting Antarctic wine.

But for now the polar plateau is still mercilessly cold, and that's something you won't encounter. All you're getting to know on this expedition is the very tip of the continent, but I can assure you that will knock your thermal socks off! Grateful, persistent applause. If only school had been half as much fun, a man compliments me on his way out—but as I write this a few hours later I can no longer picture his face. The chance to talk about ice, even just twice a day, reconciles me at least for the moment with the demise of my glacier.

In the sunny warmth of the dining room I am surrounded by laid-back voices. Ricardo is guarding the entrance to the restaurant beside his desk, he consults his register and waves me away: "I hate to tell you but there's no place for you," there are fewer seats than passengers, he's sorry, but the problem was unforeseeable. An older lady rises and offers me a place at her table, in Swiss-accented German she explains that her husband will be staying in their cabin because he isn't feeling well. Ricardo hastens to reassure the lady that he was only joking, and shoos me off to the table for the lecturers. A few passengers nod my way, by the end of the trip most will greet me by name. My response is friendly, I have no trouble being polite, I don't despise the passengers, even if Paulina insists I really do, I know from experience that the insights they will gain during the next few days will put them in a more reverent mood, but does that mean I should ignore the fact that this reverence will dissipate as soon as they're back home, that they aren't about to renounce their comfortable lifestyle, despite all the harm it causes? You're so strict when it comes to judging other people, says Paulina, as if they had personally disappointed you. If everyone was just like me, she says, I'm sure some things might be better, but some things would also be worse. "Even with people I don't like," she says, her voice getting agitated, "I always know they have their good side, I just haven't discovered it yet." For her, reality is something that has to be accepted.

At the buffet I help myself to a few appetizers and a little salad. The more I get used to this cold warm sweet buffet, the harder it is for me to decide. Instead of hardtack and herring there's an abundant assortment of food on large trays and chafing dishes, as multicolored as the flags displayed in front of a five-star hotel (everything revolves around eating, we might not be able to make a landing, the entire continent might vanish in the fog, but it's unthinkable that a meal might be canceled). During my first weeks on board—and this was my first cruise ship experience—I tried to compensate for years of missed mealtimes and quick snacks by stuffing myself with one course after another, the bounteous table offered some weak comfort, I ate and ate, fattening myself up, and ultimately realized that the more I continued to eat, the more unrestrainedly I would continue to indulge, I foresaw a fiasco of a finale, every pot pouring forth sweet and sour porridge that I had no choice but to consume, serving after endless serving, with no recourse or release in sight until I burst. He who wishes to escape the merciless force of excess supply must flee into strict frugality. A spoonful of corn, a spoonful of tuna, a spoonful of shrimp with melon, a few quartered tomatoes, a handful of pitted black olives. Naturally there's a seat in the dining room for the expedition leader, at the same table as the lecturers. There are days when I'd rather have lunch with Paulina, but unfortunately only the Brahmins are allowed such close contact with the passengers, the lower castes have to eat below decks, some will finish the entire trip without the passengers ever laying eyes on them. May I quote you? El Albatros spoons out his soup and looks at me over his tilted soup bowl. "Pardon?" "That last sentence of yours, 'And in the end the murmuring waters will fall silent, for what will wrest the ocean's secrets if not the ice,' I'd like to use that sentence."

"You listened to my lecture?"

"The end of it."

"I'll give it to you."

"Don't worry, your copyright is guaranteed."

"Copyright? What are you talking about? There's no copyright here in Terra Nullius."

"I'm planning to quote you on the rest of the planet."

El Albatros puts down his soup, and I feel something welling up inside me that I would have earlier called brotherhood. The ornithologist owes his nickname to Jeremy, who can devour untold quantities of salad and who spends the rest of the year in San Diego outfitting hiking expeditions with ultralight backpacks and tents.

"Have you ever just missed a plane and then felt this kind of existential urge to feel like you've been chosen somehow and wished that the plane would crash?"

Jeremy has finished his salad, which gives him the opportunity to record our reactions with his video camera. He besieges us with questions for his visual logbook, which he has christened *Daily Turbulences* but no one says anything. Beate comes back from the buffet and looks at the group in amazement.

"Keeping silent behind my back, eh?"

"We were just listening to Jeremy complain about not being God."

"God?" Jeremy jumps back in. "That role's already taken, what's more it's badly cast, and all the reruns in the world won't help."

"I'm much more interested," says Beate, "in hearing who would rather be reborn as an animal and who would prefer coming back as a robot."

El Albatros is the first to respond. "I'm exempt from that one," he says, "since you made me a bird in this life."

The nickname just happened to slip out of Jeremy's mouth one day after hearing yet another panegyric on the magnificent white creature with the greatest wingspan of all. He gave it an odd pronunciation, saying the "El" like a Chicano, and extending the "Albatros" just like the bird extends its wings. As soon as they've finished lunch, El Albatros rounds up all the birders like a guru gathering his sect. They are immediately recognizable from the powerful binoculars they carry around their necks, they crowd together on the open afterdeck and stare out intently, propping their elbows on the rail to steady their scopes, collecting sighting after sighting as they get soaked by the spray. One of them has taken his post behind a spotting glass, hoping to add a "lifer" to his list, a first look at a south polar skua, easily mistaken for a brown skua but a lot more rare. There's a clear sense of competition (supposedly they are inclined to compare their eyesight as they twitch away), and it's easy to get knocked off course when there's so much ambition-fueled headwind, even El Albatros has been convicted of an overly hasty misidentification. Later they huddle over an open copy of *Birds of the Antarctic*, fingers glide over feathers, shadings trigger arguments as to which jaeger has been spotted, a mistaken attribution spoils the joy of the sighting. Once on a previous trip I positioned myself within hearing distance of the bird lovers and waited a bit before giving an excited shout:

"There, over there, sooty albatross!" (I had picked out this particular rare bird earlier in the library.)

"Where, where?"

I poked my finger in the air:

"Over there"—their torsos leaned forward—"oh, now it's dived"—and they peered into the waves—"now I don't see it anymore"—and they let their gaze glide over the water—"now it's gone"—they didn't give up easily and kept scanning sea and sky with dogged tenacity—"what a shame, what a real shame."

El Albatros inquired with genuine interest about the head plumage and whether the primary feathers showed any darkened patches, I played the unsure witness until a twinkle in my eye gave me away and El Albatros forced me to confess: I can declare with absolute certainty that I have seen a striated tabular iceberg but I couldn't say for sure that I had just sighted that rare bird. El Albatros wasn't really mad at me, in fact he shares my antipathy for those passengers more interested in their checklists than in the wonder of a single bird, the miracle of its capacity to glide for hours, the marvel of its nasal salt glands, its astounding ability to dive and its mastery of navigation. Instead they fuss over recording every sighting, the place the time the witnesses, so that historians may one day draw on their extensive documentation to reconstruct the former distribution of diverse bird species on the planet. No, it won't come to that, the historians will die out before the last bird does.

Do our nightmares change—our collective nightmares? The distillate of our drunken disputes? Are nightmares the most honest expression of any given era? During his sleep my father used to lose his way in a snowstorm (as he confessed to me one day as proof of his affection), he would stumble blindly across a house that had no doors or windows or chimney but which was inhabited, the house smelled of life (stuffed cabbage rolls—that's how culinarily precise my father's nightmares were). The building gave off warmth that thawed his frozen hands, and when he put his ear to the wooden outer wall he could hear muffled voices. But no matter how loud he cried out or even if he drummed on the wall until his hands bled, the people inside didn't hear him, or else they heard him and ignored him. His instinct for self-preservation woke him up before he perished outside that pitiless place. If only I were granted a nightmare like that, I would shout with joy, I would fling my cap into a flurry of snow, anything would be better than sitting on a cliff with a clump of ice melting in my hands, leaking water that trickles down my arms and into my shirt and over my thighs, dripping and dripping into a puddle between my legs. No matter how carefully I cradle the ice in my hands it continues to melt. I try to stash it somewhere, set it on a cliff, but the ice stays glued to my hands until in the end all I'm holding is a sopping relic, a souvenir. What a disgustingly sentimental dream, I can imagine my colleagues' blank reaction, Hölbl would give me a lambasting, they've really gone and dumped some shit in your subconscious, he would say. There are some night-mares you cannot entrust to anyone.

••• — — •••

It's hard for me to say anything about it, mamma mia, enjoy it while supplies last, tutti frutti, I'm sorry but I can't seem to locate your reservation, no we're all booked up, I'm afraid there isn't a room to be had in the whole town, we have fallen victim to flattery, hey are those knockers of yours insured, works of art like that must be worth untold fortunes, he who destroys nature is killing God, that's how my neighbor put it, he's taking this cruise in the Antarctic, you know the drill, so swing over to our website pantanddrooldotcom, you can count on our webcam to deliver the goods, as soon as the Antarctic becomes an emerging market we'll open an office there, in other words, Your Excellency, do we live in theocidal times? we have to wake him, in such cases the Foreign Minister must be informed at once, I'll tell him about the matter right away. All ravens are black as pitch, offhand I can't say for certain, but it does appear somewhat exaggerated, thrill dee dill, my pretty poof, sooner or later our hour will strike, those are measurements to die for, unbelievable, and here's a job that's worth an entire future. Make it absolutely clear that we don't know if we're looking at an accident or a crime, and don't forget to mention that a terrorist attack cannot be ruled out at this time. You don't expect you can just go strolling through the palm trees scot-free do you, I'm paying taxes on expenses I reject, no one's going to question it except the ones writing the questions, imfao greed is a worse sin than waste, let's assume all living things had the same spirit, the same soul but different bodies, it's now or never, that's sick! well yes, it's completely sick, don't exaggerate, it's pathologically sick! you old geezer, beyond healing and beyond hope, do you have it in a smaller size? Does your memory stray to a brighter summer day, the situation can't be all that bad, the reason for the season time to try a toothsome threesome. We all believe that there's a good way out, last week we barely squeaked by an environmental disaster, at the time everybody talked about drawing the proper conclusions from the catastrophe. Sittin' in the morning sun, what I don't know won't hurt me, a real storybook career, from model to moderator, you can't raise a stink about that, BREAKING NEWS HUNDREDS NARROWLY ESCAPE DEATH? HUNDREDS NARROWLY ESCAPE DEATH? nothing will help except a complete reboot

• • • — — • • •

4.

51°41'37"S, 57°49'15"W

THIS TIME, TOO, it's raining in the Falklands. Days when it doesn't rain go into the annals, as do evenings when the darts don't fly in the Victory Bar. Life in Stanley used to be full of unexpected danger, people could cut peat at will above the town, water would collect in the holes, until one night a mudslide sluiced into the sleeping city without waking a single dog, swallowing house after house and sweeping school and church into the harbor and suffocating a shopkeeper and two shearers. That also went into the annals. Years ago the governor let it be known that Stanley was a very British town on a very British island (cruise ship lecturers take note of such pithy remarks, they enjoy assembling such sayings for their own use). The governor merits contradicting: in actuality the islands belong to South Africa, geologically speaking (my claim), biologically they are part of South America (Beate's view), politically they belong to Great Britain

and to Great Britain alone (Margaret Thatcher's position). The passengers bombard us with questions about
the war, one of the rare wars between white men, they
remember the tense evenings in front of the television. I
always answer short and to the point: it was the first war in
the history of the Western Hemisphere in which more
humans died than animals. I have no idea if that's true,
animals seldom make it into war reports, but it does shock
the passengers.

Paulina has been wanting to go on an outing. We've
never taken a walk together on British soil. Up to now
we've only landed on the Falklands when the trip was
nearing its end, Paulina was busy taking inventory, and
I was preparing the auction of memorabilia on behalf of
a foundation whose mission it is to teach fishermen ways
to keep their longlines from killing hundreds of thousands of albatrosses every year. But now we have a good
afternoon hour all to ourselves. She puts on apple-green
shoes and an oversized raincoat, which billows out in
the wind like a racing sail, I have to hold her arm so she
doesn't fly away. We take off, just the two of us, in the
direction of Gypsy Cove, along a waterlogged path I
know that follows the windswept shore close to the water,
our steps and voices startle a covey of ducks, Falkland
steamer ducks, I announce with the voice of expert
conviction, Paulina laughs and points to the wreck of
the *Lady Elizabeth*.

"That's a pretty big steamer duck right there."

"Ok, ok, I was fibbing, in reality they're Argentine stiff
tails."

"And I'm supposed to believe that, Professor? Don't you go pulling my leg. And I suppose those are British boobies?"

"Certainly not, those are coots. Adult white-winged coots, I swear it."

Her hands have found a path through the layers of wind and rain protection, past Gore-Tex and wool, and she strokes my chest with life-affirming coldness.

"You're the one who taught me," she says with windy seriousness, "that people who know a lot lie the most."

"Could we agree on the word 'invent'?"

My appeal is tendered halfheartedly, the path veers away from the shore and takes us across a low shrubby heath strewn with stones and on toward Yorke Bay (some of the passengers are headed our way, judging from the way they're staring at us I can only imagine what they are thinking). A ranger is standing next to a wooden shelter, as though he were waiting just for us to deliver his explanations. Paulina jabs her finger in my direction and says to the ranger: "If you only knew what this evil man . . ."

The ranger presses his lips together and raises his eyebrows, I nip the coming irritation in the bud.

"It's not half as bad as it sounds, we just couldn't agree on which birds had which names."

"You have a wonderful beach here, people must love it."

"Yes, it's the most beautiful beach in town."

"And not a soul in sight, in my country it would be overflowing with romping children and passed-out parents on a friendly Saturday like this."

"I wouldn't advise that."

"On account of the current?"

"Not because of the ocean, the beach itself is deadly dangerous."

"How so?"

"It's mined."

"Mined?"

"Antipersonnel mines."

"I don't understand, the place is swarming with penguins."

"Your question is entirely justified, ma'am, but consider that the mines require a weight of twenty kilos to explode, and even a fully grown Magellan penguin doesn't get that big, so you may rest assured that the animals have nothing to fear."

Paulina puts her hand to her mouth.

"Soldiers make the best animal protectors," I say.

"It was the Argentines," the ranger specifies.

"Just like in my country," says Paulina, "everything looks like paradise until the bullets start whizzing past your ears."

She laughs again, but this time it's a different laugh, the kind she uses to wipe away something unpleasant.

"They like it here, the Magellan penguins, they dig their nest burrows in the soft peaty soil up there in the dune grass."

"They dig their nests?"

"Yes ma'am, and they use the burrows for years, they mate for life and never separate. They pick their partners carefully and can rely on them completely."

We listen to his lecture, and to the oyster fishermen in the background, then take our leave and head off into the blooming furze, where I pick some mouse-eared chickweed, "not for you, Paulina, it's for the family altar in our cabin, for all the grandmothers." On the way back we stop at one of the fence posts that has a red sign nailed to it, at closer distance we can make out a skull and crossbones below the words "Danger Mines."

At the counter in the reception someone left a brochure which I open in passing. "The Falkland Islands are one of the few places in the world where nature reigns supreme." A minefield as unspoiled nature? Why not, after all, Kitzbühel counts as a climatic health resort even on holidays with bumper-to-bumper traffic jams. All El Albatros has to spare for me is contradiction. If all beaches were mined we wouldn't have to worry about bird refuges. I listen to him with one ear, at the next table over some men are talking as they spoon their crème brûlée about the charming heather moor at Yorke Bay, ideal for a golf course, a classic links, and while they let their fantasies go teeing off I imagine how in the course of construction the location of the landmines might be forgotten. A beach like that ("a spectacular par 3 shot right over the heads of our native Magellanic penguins") could become the ultimate sand trap, one which could rightly be billed as a bunker you might never get out of.

I've been watching it my entire life, with passionate care and precise instruments. And if my observations will have had no impact on my chosen field and how this field views itself, then my academic career will have been a waste. Every May and September I would go a few days ahead of my students, so I could abandon myself to my senses, undisturbed, and feel the glacier's full emotional force before we captured its data. It was my doctoral advisor who placed this particular glacier in my care, an arranged marriage that in time became a union of love, as if every measurement were an acknowledgment of its singularity. On that first morning I rose before the sun, laced up my hiking boots which initially felt strange, and then I trekked around the glacier, ascending on the left side and then after crossing the ice descending below the escarpment on the other side. Each time I visited I would first scan the glacier with my eyes, then test it with my feet. Whenever I stopped to catch my breath I would touch it, laying my hands on its flanks and then stroking my face, taking in its icy breath, its invigorating cold. I was familiar with every one of its sounds, the creaking and the clanking, every glacier has its own voice, when I visited others I would compare theirs with the one I knew. A dying glacier sounds different than a healthy one, it gives off a powerful rattle when it bursts along a crevasse, and if you listen closely you can hear the melt flowing into the underground lakes speeding the erosion of the wrinkled body. We were like an elderly couple: one of us was severely ill, and the other couldn't do anything about it. All terms used to describe our relationship—such as "subject of study" or "mass balance measurement"—were woefully inadequate, and no column of figures could do any more justice to my devotion than could our bookkeeping, which recorded the snowfall deposit at the end of the winter as a kind of revenue, and the degree of summer thaw as a kind of expense. These credits and debits caused me greater and greater despair, and over the years I changed into a kind of doctor who had only to look into the eyes of his patient to make the proper diagnosis. I recognized that my glacier was doomed long before the declining values of its middle layer thickness pronounced their judgment. I didn't have to wait for the results to understand the ramifications of the sustained depletion. It was no longer possible to offset the loss. We were aging together, the glacier and I, but the glacier was well ahead of me when it came to dying.

Rules, rules, and more rules. Without strict guidelines people would trample over everything, I see that, at the same time it's humiliating for me to have to force rules on them. One of the least pleasant among my new tasks involves corralling the press. There are always a few journalists on board—the cruise line appreciates the relatively inexpensive advertising in their articles—as well as a handful of relaxed editors and pushy photographers. On the last trip of the previous season there were a dozen, the expedition leader wanted a silent partner sitting in on the meetings to bolster his authority and that's when I first learned of this duty. Journalists don't have any special privileges either on board the ship or on land, the idea has to be put out of their head at the start. My predecessor took a strict tone, to me it sounded like the tinny parody of a politician's call for law and order, I had to suppress a

smile and turn away, as though I were expecting something surprising out of the west-southwest. "Is there something you want to tell me?" he asked afterwards.

"Do we have to treat them like they're educationally
challenged?"

"When it comes to dealing with nature, as far as I'm
concerned every person on the planet is educationally
challenged," answered the expedition leader who is now
lying in a hospital room in Buenos Aires, where he is
presumably studying his yachting magazines as attentively
as I am studying the faces of the journalists who have gathered around me in a semicircle and who are introducing
themselves one by one at my invitation. That gives me a
chance to separate the chaff from the wheat, the insightful
from the unruly. I form my judgments hastily, instinctively.
How is it that the Roman ideal of presumed innocence has
endured in our civilization so pervaded with the notion of
original sin? The boisterous blonde from Hamburg won't
cause any trouble, she's brought her boyfriend along for a
working vacation, she'll avoid anything that might make
her seem unpleasant. The Colombian cameraman has
eyes that suggest an easily ignited insolence, while his
accompanying editor gives off an air of laziness, I'm sure he
won't be stirring up anything provocative. The striking
young American is clearly nervous and this makes her also
seem unapproachable. "I'm Mary from *Mother Jones* and
please no wisecracks." I look around, wondering what she
is alluding to, but nobody seems to get the supposedly obvious joke. I'm certain that the muscular cameraman, who
probably wears his dignified smile even in his sleep, will try

his luck with her by sharing some hastily concocted witti-
cism as soon as they leave the lecture room. The last in line
is a smart-suited man who introduces himself as Dan
Quentin's PR manager and then pauses for a moment as if
he were expecting a show of admiring smiles and glances
that to my astonishment are indeed accorded, apparently
I'm the only one who doesn't fully appreciate the name.
His own business requires a special discussion, as the
captain has undoubtedly informed me. Evidently the man
is paid to find the right words to maneuver himself into a
privileged position. "No," I answer, "the captain and I
haven't had any time to confer about Dan Quentin, but
I'm certain we'll have that opportunity, for now though I'd
like to agree on a few basics. In a word, the same rules
apply to journalists as to all other passengers on this cruise.
Never leave the paths marked with red flags, never pull
anything out of the ground, don't take anything and don't
throw anything away, not even the tiniest shred of paper.
Always keep a distance of at least five meters from all
animals, penguins included, and don't try to blame it on
the poor penguins not knowing the rules, we've heard that
excuse more than once. Like all other passengers you may
spend no more than two hours on land, don't try to carve
out any more time. And follow our instructions, if you don't
then we'll have to leave you behind and you can write a
feature about surviving the winter all alone that will make
you world famous." Scarcely have I spoken these words
than I begin to doubt whether my approach is any better
than that of my predecessor. Then I ask if everyone understood what I just said; after all when people are speaking a

second or third language there's a greater risk of misunderstanding. Dan Quentin's manager chews on his sunglasses, Mary writes everything down, the editor has the cameraman translate the last portion of my speech in whispered tones (shouldn't the editor be the one with a better command of English?). Any questions? There aren't any, because everyone is distracted by what is drifting past. "Aha, the first iceberg," I try out a lighter tone, but now no one is paying attention, "in two weeks you'll have seen so many icebergs you won't even turn your head when one shows up." As expected, just after my parting words the manager jumps up and runs over and starts speaking at me while he's still moving, as if I were a typewriter on which he were urgently typing a letter requesting payment. He asks me to speak with the captain as soon as I can, it's about a project that's so colossal the logistical demands cannot be underestimated, the artistic vision is explosive and amazingly timely, the Antarctic has now become a project in the hearts of all mankind, Dan Quentin wants to create a sign, he wants to hoist an emotional flag that will be seen across the globe, a symbol for danger and endangerment, he wants to coin a highly original visual currency. Tomorrow after breakfast the manager will come to see me, he's looking forward to our collaboration. In the meantime Mary has kept in the background, now she breaks away and asks shyly if she might ask me for an interview when I have a free hour. Gratefully I agree.

My students didn't know what an oxbow is. Some thought it had to do with pastures, others with plowing tools. They weren't even embarrassed by their ignorance, as if they had a fundamental right to forget about what has been destroyed. Over breakfast on the last day of our summer stay at the glacier I asked them to pack their things before we climbed up for our last visit, and paid the proprietor of Zum Kogl a hundred schillings to deliver the luggage to the station in time for our train. After we had completed one final hike around the glacier I suggested that we make the first part of our return trip on foot. They asked why, and I explained that was the only way to really read a landscape. A few grumbled, but no one dared stay at the bus stop—the ongoing need to prove oneself is a powerful corrective. We gazed down into the valley. From above, the effect of human intervention is quite visible, it's easy to see what we have done to nature. That was hardly a revelation, even for the students conditioned by city living who didn't know what an oxbow was. I wanted them to spend at least one afternoon seeing with their own eyes, consciously observing the shrinking fens, the straightened rivers, our civilization's attempts to impose its own discipline on the natural world. From one ledge where the valley opened up below us like an accordion file, I gave a short lecture about the river meadows as they used to be, until people started thinking of them as worthless land, like alien beings that had wandered into their anthropometric order and needed taming, which is why what we are looking at is land that has been drained and cleared and made useful, where the wet meadows have given way to apple orchards. First the natural state was wiped clean, then cultivation was introduced. But among hundreds of varieties of apple there are only a few that meet the reigning market standards — standards that doom any unregulated growth to failure. Taste and color are determined by chemical analysis. With the screen of our simplemindedness we have managed to sift out all natural variety. I closed my extemporaneous speech telling about a local farmer who a few years earlier was blessed with the tastiest harvest he'd ever had, but he'd been unable to sell because the size and shape of his fruit didn't correspond to the supermarket norms, he was stuck with a rotting pile of apples he would have gladly given away if enough children had come by. A while later, when we stopped by an Alpine pasture for a snack, several of the students pulled polished Granny Smiths out of their backpacks, they looked at their standardized apples and exchanged embarrassed glances. As they bit into the fruit they may have wondered what a proper apple really tasted like. In one or two cases this curiosity might turn into a persistent yearning, but it would be foolhardy to hope for anything beyond that.

The pianist is waiting for me, very impatient. He always acts as though he's bothered by my mere presence, but whenever I'm late he looks around to see where I might be, and if I keep him waiting longer he asks Erman the bartender for my whereabouts. After dinner we digest the day. I function as his discursive GPS, by referencing my own position in contrast to his, he is able to determine his coordinates. I ask if the Falklands make him feel a flash of patriotic pride, but he refuses to be baited. "The only beautiful women on this godforsaken island," he answers, "are the Thai ladies in the souvenir shop." Far from wasting his thirty years aboard cruise ships on touristic nonsense, the pianist has undertaken an extensive study of womanhood in a variety of habitats. As far as he's concerned, women who hail from distant lands are the last wilderness on earth (when we're alone he regales me with ribaldries that would certainly elicit an indignant huff from Mrs. Morgenthau). Like all connoisseurs he appreciates the uncommon, the unusual, the outlandish. If he ever retires—and I doubt he will, because for all his British chauvinism, which gets freshly creased and ironed every day, he is secretly afraid of English provincial life— he will undoubtedly relay his philogynous experiences in tones befitting such a man of the world. "By the way," I say, "the beach is still mined." He raises his gin and tonic, flips the coaster over with his left hand and places the glass irritatingly in the middle of the table. He seems excited, he has something up his sleeve, something he wants to tease me with, he can scarcely wait. I close my eyes. Behind me I hear clinking sounds as voices fill glasses, glasses run over, voices rinse the glasses out, I feel an acidic wave rising from the depths of my stomach. When I reopen my eyes the pianist is leaning forward and speaking in a conspiratorial voice: "If you only knew what was lying on the bottom of the ocean."

"Gold?" I guess without enthusiasm. "Torpedos? Giant fan worms?"

"Nothing of the kind. Ships, powerful ships. And any number of compatriots."

"Whose compatriots?"

"Yours."

He leans back in his chair.

"I understand they've been here a while?"

"Ever since the First World War."

"I'm not interested, we let that one go a long time ago, these days we're more interested in fresher corpses." The pianist nods, as if my reply was as easy to predict as the next move in a classic chess opening.

"Does the name Admiral Graf von Spee mean anything to you?"

"No, nothing, wait, von Spee . . . von Spee? When I was a student I used to live near a square called Graf-Spee-Platz."

"Undoubtedly named after the same man. A prominent admiral."

"Does he have a von in his name or not?"

"That's immaterial. The fact is he's one of your heroes."

"And how exactly was he heroic?"

"He crossed two oceans and then showed up here in Stanley with his entire fleet, having got it in his head he would interrupt the British coal supply, even though he knew that he was hopelessly outgunned."

The pianist's voice whirred on, now he could take his hands off the handlebars, it was all downhill from here, an easy ride to his goal.

"At the time, Stanley was excellently protected by two battle cruisers, the H.M.S. *Invincible* and the H.M.S. *Inflexible* . . ."

"That was a very gentlemanly gesture, to give Admiral Graf von Spee such a clear warning."

"Gentlemanly indeed, but it was of little avail, your Admiral ignored their presence and insisted on going down in these waters, together with two thousand hands including two of his own sons."

"A cold grave. And what are you trying to tell me with this story?"

"For a geologist you are remarkably impatient. Before the battle, the squadron at a bay in southern Chile, that cost time, the element of surprise was lost, but it had to be: the admiral insisted on pinning Iron Crosses on three hundred of his sailors."

"Are you telling me that three hundred Iron Crosses are lying just off the Falklands?"

"You're catching on."

"That's insane."

"On the contrary, it makes perfect sense, the farsighted admiral anticipated his demise and wanted to make sure his men did not go down undecorated."

The pianist rested one arm on the back of the crimson chair and looked at me with great satisfaction. He has a remarkable talent for staging his own well-contented state, he smacked his lips and ran a finger along the rim of his gin-and-tonic glass, now nearly empty.

"Crosses on the sea bottom, mines on the beach, I have to admit I might have underestimated your island a bit."

"Next time we should go for a walk together."

"I'll mull it over. But only if you take my request this evening."

"Just don't be too hard on me, I don't know any Germanic funeral marches."

"I'd never dream of asking for something like that. I'm thinking of something more current, something you could play with your left hand while unbuttoning a summer dress with your right."

"Now you're talking."

"In honor of Admiral Graf von Spee, in honor of the light-footed penguins on the beach I would like to hear the only song I feel would do the occasion justice."

"Aha, now you're giving in."

"What I'd very much like to hear is *Rule Britannia! Britannia rule the waves.*"

At least one time on every trip the talk turns to the hundred Inuit names for ice and snow. I always confirm that it's true, the Inuit have a name for ice floe, pancake ice, hummocked ice, brash ice and grease ice, tabular iceberg, ice cliff, ice needles, ice foot and ice tongue, for the ice fields formed out of firn, for ice caps, permanent ice, ice age and for growlers and bergy bits. But I'm not one hundred percent sure they have a word for glacier fleas.

••• — — •••

Like an elephant in a china shop, nothing's as bad as it looks, things have gotten out of balance, you can write that one off, below 40° S there is no law, snap yours up now while supplies last, you've just begun to scratch the surface, November Zulu. This is Foxtrot Two Niner, over. This is November Zulu, proceed, Foxtrot Two

Niner, over. I'm flying back from Gerlache Strait, over.
What's going on? over. Dan Quentin, over. Dan who?
over. You can squeeze out a little more, no one's going
to question it, the guru chose the peace and solitude of
the mountains, Charlie we haven't paid her ass the trib-
ute it deserves, I don't have eyes in the back of my head,
ha ha ha, you didn't see that, in the spring, summer and
fall months he lived in the dense forest, his only roof was
heaven. Quentin's raking it in, he's the new Christo,
over. Roger, never heard of this Dan Quentin, what does
he have to do with Christ? over. Christo, The Umbrellas,
Valley Curtain, Running Fence, over. Doesn't mean a
thing to me, over. Making nature visible by covering it
up, over. That's an old whore's trick, over. Art with
people, over. Torch them all, every SUV, give the fire-
bugs a field day, under no circumstances should you
mention that in your job interview, first there's a big
bang then the car bursts into flame, in winter he retreated
to a cave that protected him from ice and snow, below
$50°$ S there is no government, whatever had been sown
and reaped by human hands he refused to eat. For example, over? "FAQ" in Silicon Valley, "QED" in the Burj
Khalifa, over. The naked cyclists in Hyde Park? over.
That was somebody else, over. What's he looking for in
the Antarctic? over. A big SOS on ice, over. He collected
fruit from wild trees, plants from the forest and roots
from the earth, below $60°$ S there is no god, we got off
with a black eye, he fed his body just what he needed to
survive. The passengers on board the *Hansen* linked
together to form a red SOS, over. By choice? over. Yes,

about a hundred pax per letter. It was a show, I'm telling you, out. Roger, out. I will fulfill all of your desires BREAKING NEWS MS HANSEN HIJACKED IN THE ANTARCTIC BREAKING NEWS MS HANSEN HIJACKED IN THE ANTARCTIC I'll be sittin' when the evening comes

●●● ━ ━ ●●●

5.

53°11′8″S, 45°22′4″W

STANDING BRACED ON the weather deck of a pitching cruise ship, taking in the gale, the storm, face lashed by wind and spray, having the breath knocked out of the lungs, at the mercy of the elements and frozen through after only a few minutes no matter how many layers of high-end high-tech material — passengers can enjoy a brief taste of the deprivations of a bygone era, just one door removed from the warm cabin from where they can witness nature unleash its force through a glass pane as though they were watching a prizewinning documentary. Almost everyone chooses the comfortable front-row view. Alone at the bow I lean over the railing, the spray spits in my face, I claw myself into the wood, the wind slaps my cheeks, it has every right to punish me for my comfort, for the deadly sin of a civilization bent on denying the basic principle of life, because whatever lives must strive to climb the energy gradient. Petrels dance among the gusts, the ecstasy of their soaring and diving is my own yearning taken wing, I rock in the air as if I, too, had been granted such ability, the engines burble away in the maw of the howling storm, how ridiculous am I to be impressed by the obvious. We cannot read the flight of birds, says El Albatros, merely misunderstand it. In the half-visibility I sense the outline of a mighty object, an iceberg is floating our way, it's larger than our ship, flat on top as though brushed smooth, as if an entire province had detached from the shelf ice and was damned to orbit the South Pole or drift north and expire, bequeathing to the hemisphere the purest air, and to the ocean the cleanest water, laden with healing powers that enable the phytoplankton to grow, as well as the zooplankton that sustain the small shrimp-like krill that nurture birds and whales (Beate claims that within her lifetime the krill population has declined by four fifths, there's no arguing about it). The ice has been punched with oval holes, mighty vulvas pushing deep inside the berg. Melting mating calls. Behind a curtain of mist the sun flares unexpectedly, a measure of mortality. The glow withstands a few more waves before it disappears again and the storm rages on in the twilight.

Could this be calm? A commodity precious enough to be marketed with enormous success, guarded in protected areas, sheltered in reserves. But these ecological niches are shrinking as the pulse of our age thuds on ahead in four-quarter time.

One day some years back, just after the church bells rang vespers, I said I had no desire to go out and eat in some pub where they drench the roast venison in an earsplitting sauce.

"Does that mean you're not going to the doctor because they play Radio Bavaria in the waiting room?" Helene asked full of spite. "And what about the dentist and all his spherical sounds straight from the Buddha?"

She snatched the car keys from the ceramic dish and rushed off to her sister, who was well inclined toward me because she didn't have the patience for Helene's continuous loop of complaint. I sat down on the chair in the hallway, closed my eyes and stayed there a long time. How did it happen that words like "quiet" and "standstill" have turned into something pejorative? Even on hiking trails I hear the numbing bass notes of music junkies who can no longer bear the sound of nature. If they at least just listened to their own voices, but no, they have to smear a layer of stale noise over every single thing. Admittedly I also put on a pair of headphones now and then in the S-Bahn on the way to the university, Thomas Tallis did a lot to help mask the ugliness of the utility buildings along the way, but it would have been unthinkable to listen to his music in the woods or on the mountain or when I was with people I knew. The *Hansen* doesn't have a public address system (unlike other ships in other latitudes, where according to Paulina jingles screech and fanfares boom). Recently they held a rock concert on King George Island, soon the glacial faces will come tumbling down like the walls of Jericho. In our cabin the only perceptible sound is Paulina's tender singing (in contrast to many of her compatriots she isn't glued to her iPhone); she mixes evergreen hits from the '70s with Filipino folk tunes. In fact it was her singing that cast me in a spell on the last evening of my first trip, I had hardly noticed her before that, her unobtrusive politeness blended in with the ready friendliness of all the other Filipinos. But at the farewell concert—the passengers had given the crew a chance to amuse themselves—she metamorphosed into a confident chanteuse, a bundle of energy inside a cone of light, she crossed her legs and let her right shoe slide down her foot so only the silver buckle was looped over her toe, the shoe dangled and swayed and all desires were fixed on her as she sang the old hits to a plucked accompaniment with an intensity that let me draw a curtain shutting the two of us off from the rest of the world. Later my feverish fantasy made me self-conscious as we stood next to each other at the after-party in the cafeteria, I was certain she could sense me looking at her with different eyes, my desire mixed with a strong dose of insecurity, my tongue my best enemy, and nevertheless a few hours later she lay next to me, just like now, with her head on my shoulder and one hand on my chest, and as so often on our days on the open sea, when one or the other of us is granted a free hour, she has asked me to read something out loud to her. I am happy to comply, for me it is a gesture of intimacy, I read a passage from the reports of the so-called Explorers because of her charming compassion for the hardships and suffering they faced, though in my anger I see them less as pioneers and more as avaricious parvenus seeking to take possession of the Antarctic as if she were a virgin who after the first night was theirs by right for all other nights, and so they despised all competitors as thieving rivals, while they themselves sought to conceal their own lust so as not to endanger their spotless reputation as impeccable gentlemen.

"It only seems that way to you," says Paulina after a pause that she occasionally asks for so she can keep up with the story, "because that's how you read it, your anger is seeping into their words, but you're really just like they are, you want to determine what happens to the Antarctic."

My voice flares up. "If you mean I don't want any people or fuel oil in the Antarctic, then you're right, I do want to determine what happens here. But I don't want to possess the place, that's the difference, I don't want to have any part of it named after me, I just want it to be left in peace."

Paulina pouts and wrinkles her nose. "You get so loud. You know, sometimes you can be a very loud person." She hardly seems vulnerable and in need of protection when she challenges me like that, when she puts me in my place with simple sentences that make my replies seem inappropriately exaggerated. And that just makes me madder, the fact that I have a hard time explaining what I perceive and fear and despise, even to her. It's plain as day, our profit-driven turpitude, why is it so hard for me to express the obvious to those who don't see it? Just look at the picture, do you see a beautiful young woman or a wrinkled old woman? And once you've seen the wrinkled old woman will you ever be able to make out the beautiful young one? I turn away from Paulina, pompously wallowing in my anger like an elephant seal in his mudhole, until I've calmed down again. "My dear Paulina," I whisper to her in sorrow and distress, "you are as much a mystery to me as the world itself," and she beams, presumably because of the my dear Paulina, her smile lingers, a little happiness goes a long way with her, she consumes her blessings sparingly, while others need a new ration every day. I can't imagine that any real lasting strife might come between us and settle in the narrow space of our cabin, she senses intuitively where I am reconcilable, the first time it happened unexpectedly, I was frightened, she took my rage inside her mouth and cooled it off so that we both grew silent. Later I stroked her little belly and said, "This makes you complete," and she answered, "You make me complete"—a sentence I would never let her get away with if her laughter didn't start to boil over again and seethe. Her quaking stomach arouses me, she takes the book from my hands and sets it down where moments later I toss her underwear, I forgive every sentence, and in order not to say any more wrong things I silence my voice with an eager tongue, my hands placed on her breasts, even when the ship's rolling nearly knocks me down, my tongue circles on, stoking her passion, so that it doesn't fade, the sea swells set the rhythm and in my mind she tastes of salt while drifting through my brain amid all the moaning is the question of whether we will ever be able to understand each other. What she wants is for us to simply be, while I seek deliverance in some more absolute silence.

In the summer before my glacier died, we packed up all our belongings and then unpacked them. Vacation passed and with it my desire for domesticity. Some couples get pregnant to save their relationship, Helene and I decided to move. From an apartment in Fürstenried to a single family house in Solln. She was supposed to tidy up while I spent another few days on the mountain supervising my students as they measured the degree of ablation. It was a lively group, unusually encouraging and supportive of one another, and I came back to our apartment in an upbeat mood. Not sensing anything amiss, I climbed the stairs, where I ran into the short-statured retiree from the second floor and his exceptionally unfriendly look. I unlocked the door and pushed against it with my shoulder, the wooden panel resisted, I had to press with all my weight just to make it in. A dozen moving boxes had fallen over, some were blocking the door and a few had slid onto the floor where they'd knocked down a pair of rubber boots that were lying between a halfway rolled-up sleeping mat and a torn sombrero. Helene had dismantled everything, hadn't cleaned up, and disappeared without a trace. I carefully picked my way ahead and found myself standing between remnant skeins of woolen yarn and stacks of framed prints that had been taken off the walls, which were now as naked as they'd been in my childhood home (before Oma bequeathed us her still lifes), the whole place was as jam-packed and jumbled as my room had been during summer vacation, when I took out all my toys, all the figurines and playing cards, all the tokens and dice, and spread them out on the floor and made up my own games which took place on the rug, the table, the bed. In honor of its inventor I christened these tournaments "Zeno's Olympics," and before starting I would call out into the hall: "Please don't come in my room." Helene could have at least posted a similar note on the door: "Please don't come in the apartment." The hall was crowded with open boxes whose contents were hidden by wads of crumpled newspaper, old parkas hung from the coat stand like the branches of a weeping willow, the side tables were piled high with printed matter stacked this way and that, including several years of *Burda Style* (even if Helene never sewed anything herself, she made sure to save the patterns, as models for some alternative life design), the issue on top dated from the late '70s, the mannequin on the cover had the same impressive perm as Helene did back then, leafing through I found a page that was missing a piece the size of a postcard. Would Helene really throw away all these magazines, could she let go of her collection of clippings? She kept them in large portfolios—first-aid kits she used to open whenever she was in a bad mood. When her life objectives became blurred by everyday routine she would revisit the pictures of fancy gifts, dream vacations and anti-aging products and readjust her goals. Then she would close the portfolio with a deep sigh, the kind I knew all too well, the oh-if-only-we-could sigh, until finally the day came when I started earning as a full professor. Then we went on our first dream vacation and came back covered with bug bites and sick to our stomachs, that's what happens when you book something cheap, were Helene's enlightening words (to avoid a fight I stopped myself from asking what was cheap about the most expensive trip of our lives).

From that point on she collected only offers whose price and exclusivity ruled out all risk of disappointment, and these were no longer clippings but whole catalogs with semi-glossy foldouts more lavishly produced than the Alpine photo albums that lay next to the stacks of *Burda Style*, now as out of date as the desire with which they were once filled. Helene had taken our interior life and turned it inside out, drawers cabinets chests shelves in every room had been emptied and whatever she didn't fit into a box she flung aside, creating in the process a mixed-media installation of superfluity. She seemed to be curating our entire inventory, people here all seem to inhabit their own museums nowadays. Some of the objects I had forgotten: the electric carving knife, the bread slicer, the yoghurt maker, enough shoe polish for a very shiny eternity, countless sunglasses, belts, purses. I had never noticed how many blazers Helene had acquired over the years, because after all every special occasion demanded a new blazer, they were spread out on the bed, and there were enough to form a small mound, shaped like some prehistoric grave. The Delft majolica that had once belonged to Helene's grandmother was laid out on the buffet table (tradition is that which is passed on), a few tiles were already wrapped in paper. One of the armchairs was covered with notepads and pens I had picked up at various conference hotels, while my trail maps (lightly curled souvenirs from our longest-lasting common passion) were stacked on a dining room chair, the floorboards under the table were strewn with receipts whose warranties had long expired. How could it come to this, a bedroom full of blazers, a bathroom full of firming creams, a kitchen full of Tupperware, a living room full of rocks, shells, vases, glasses from Christmas markets and wine tastings, souvenir cups ("Gruß aus Oberammergau") betwixt Mexican bowls and even a Portuguese rooster I'd been talked into buying along with the story of a roasted cock that jumped up from the judge's plate to crow the innocence of a man who was about to be hanged—how could it come to this, to our possessions driving us out of our home? And there was still the basement, where suppressed like some trauma could be found Christmas ornaments, tinsel and tree stands, rolled up handwoven rugs, three decades' worth of shoes, and multitudes of music and video cassettes, stage programs and miscellaneous folders—clearly a place to be avoided. In the apartment itself there was nowhere to sit down, every chair was laden with our belongings, the large armchair was buried under various misguided attempts at silk painting, macramé and origami. I perched on a seemingly stable tower of catalogues from the Pinakotheks Old New and Modern and sat there, my feet not even touching the floor, at a loss as to what to do, for the first time in my life I felt the fear of being buried alive. When the telephone rang (it had to be Helene explaining why she left so suddenly and when she planned to come back) I was staring at a small jar of preserves labeled in her convoluted script: "Strawberry preserves with amaretto (1989)."

The captain is not a control freak, but once he takes charge of something, everything has to be done the way he imagines, which isn't always easy because he ignores details and is so sparing with his speech it's as though words on board ship were rationed. He comes from up north in Lower Saxony, from a village near Friesoythe, apparently that explains a few things, people who know say the locals there limit themselves to one sentence per day, they start it in the morning and end it in the evening, I can't say myself, I was only once in Bremerhaven on business and once privately in Sankt Peter-Ording, to me those northern states might as well be a foreign country. Now that we've managed to survive a vertically divided Germany unscathed, as far as I'm concerned we could happily divide the country along some middle latitude. "I've got this bad feeling in my gut," says the Captain after a mumbled "good morning." The way he says "gut" makes it sound like an onomatopoeic expression for bad mood.

"You mean Dan Quentin?"

"I have this bad feeling."

"I can understand that."

"The company is keen on the idea."

"The siren call of fame."

"We don't know the man."

"His manager, on the other hand . . ."

"Gets on your nerves?"

"You might say that. Maybe he'll relax a bit once his boss arrives. When is Quentin supposed to join us?"

"King George Island, they're flying him in."

"He who would achieve much has little time," I say in an exaggeratedly nasal voice, but the Captain is immune to all irony. Even when he does speak he looks off in the distance somewhere beyond your shoulder, where some more urgent task seems to await him.

"We're supposed to give him all the help he needs."

"I take it we're supposed to do it out of love."

"Will you manage?"

"Do you expect complications?"

"It involves a lot of people."

"We can limit the number of participants."

"He wants to make the biggest SOS he can."

"But to do that he'll need our passengers."

"The biggest SOS in history."

"I assume that he's been informed of the restrictions."

"We're turning a blind eye to that."

"Are we?"

"If anyone inquires, the whole thing was an emergency preparedness exercise."

"The passengers will have to agree."

"That's your task."

"I'll tell them tomorrow about Mr. Quentin's installation."

"We'll discuss the rest another time."

After Helene moved out, when relocating to the house in Solln failed to achieve its therapeutic goal, the pictures on the walls faded into strange reminiscences. Whenever I looked at them I had the feeling I was looking through the window at some random life stored in the building across the street. I took them down one by one as I imbibed the red wine Helene's father had bequeathed to us: the old man had squirreled away these excellent bottles so that one far-off day they might help his son-in-law cope with the separation from his daughter. The pictures had left annoying outlines on the wall. Why is it that everything we do leaves an imprint (it takes a hundred years for a footprint in the Antarctic to disappear), why can't we simply glide through moments without a trace, like birds through the air? I didn't want to repaint all those walls, it was unclear how long I'd last inside them anyway. So I went into town and bought a large A3-size sketchpad and some watercolors, and started painting single letters of the alphabet onto individual sheets, after spending a long time deliberating which color to use for each. For A I chose a richly darkened yellow, like an aged Riesling, and for Z a garnet red pinot. O came out in a gray so soft it was indiscernible from more than a couple inches away. I painted one letter per day, and as soon as the paint dried I tacked the finished artwork to the wall. When at last the entire alphabet was adorning my walls I felt better in this house that I would never call "my house." The letters allowed me to believe in a new beginning, and they beckoned to me from the walls, enticing me to read. On a trip to Ladakh I'd heard of a man who had become a reading recluse and withdrawn into a single book. Twice a week he visits a sandalwood dealer who lives in a wooden house on a stone base near the Indus River, and whoever wants to hear him read can find him there. The man reads one line from his book and then takes his listeners on an exegetical journey through all possible nuances. I felt tempted to adopt the same procedure. At random I selected a book out of a faux-antiqued series devoted to ancient philosophers and began reading line by line, paragraph by paragraph, with the same concentration as the guru in Ladakh, after which I took three sips and laid the book aside. Then I stretched my legs and returned and wrote down everything I could remember of the reading. Little by little all my initial flippancy evaporated and my supply of red wine dwindled but I sipped away until I had practically memorized the entire book. According to my informants in Ladakh it takes the word-fasting guru twenty years to guide his students through that one book, whereupon he starts all over again with a new batch of followers. Despite my admiration there was something about the whole procedure that bothered me, something didn't seem to make sense. How can people consider a book holy unless they've rewritten it for their own purposes? Is it even possible for two people to mean the same thing when they say "God" or when they talk about love? At first I underlined individual words or sentences, often two or three times, I circled them, boxed them in, filling the small spaces between the lines with my observations until I realized there was no reason not to use the margins. I didn't set the book aside until it was covered with my scribbling. After that I bought this leather-bound notebook. I declined the seller's offer to have my name engraved.

And at the end of a long day on the open sea, when darkness has blackened everything, the stars grow dull, the wind breathes its last, our ship sails on into the last refuge of abundance. There is only one Terra Nullius left on

Earth, and that's where we are headed, "whiles all the night, through fog-smoke white" the language shrinks back from the miracle, the silence awaits us beyond the mist, where "glimmered the white Moon-shine."

••• — — — •••

So pick up your phone and dial right now for your chance to win, the first three callers will receive a free blow job, I'm not what you'd call happy-go-fucky, Charlie don't start without me, I've kissed the girls of Naples, as they say the pitcher will keep going to the well until it breaks, you can't afford to give things away either, Charlie, wait she's not just yours you know, do your looting while supplies last. The matter will be looked into at once, I'm afraid you're going to have to fly right back, you better eat something while the machine's being refueled, this is no longer a photo shoot, it's an emergency. They're pretty as can be, that comes from putting off the necessary repairs, the street is closed due to construction, please follow the detour, oceangoing tankers are kept in use until they break apart, see-lonce, see-lonce, watchin' the ships roll in, legs well worth the look let me tell you, where there's a middle class there will be banksters, you slave away for thirty years scrimping and saving every penny never going on vacation and then something like this happens, imao, do you have any idea what's at stake here? we're looking at a maritime emergency with international complications, all ships in the area, the *Urd*, the *Verdandi* and the *Skuld* are headed for Gerlache Strait to rescue the passengers, we have to be prepared for every contingency. You want to know the problem with the indigenous people, I'll tell you, they're too docile, we need to infect them with our greed, otherwise there'll never be any peace between them and us, the overweight will have to weigh things over. The first ship should be there in roughly two hours, the captain of the *Urd* has taken command of the operation, water doesn't get any colder. Then I watch them roll away again, you should snatch that up, the weather changes every minute and so does the business climate, and I'm sittin' on the dock of the bay, the atmospheric depressions return every thirty-six hours, watchin' the tide roll away, in the course of a single day we experience all four seasons, I'm just sittin' on the dock of the bay BREAKING NEWS HOPE FOR SURVIVORS BREAKING NEWS HOPE FOR SURVIVORS wastin' time

··· − − − ···

6.

54°16′8″S, 36°30′5″W

A DAY WHEN clouds look like mountains and mountains like clouds. Alpine peaks spring up in the middle of the ocean, a tear in the sloping cloudbank exposes rocky cliffs and glaciers looming over patches of pasture, where reindeer introduced by homesick Norwegians chomp away at the vegetation. Trees have never set down their roots. The water inside the pot cove is rich in oxygen and krill and takes on a greenish tint. Here Creation appears with unfamiliar clarity, as though all cataracts have been removed and our collective vision was suddenly unclouded. We put into Grytviken, an old whaling station that was abandoned overnight and left to rot and ruin. The passengers stroll from the cemetery to the flensing plan to the mudhole where the elephant seals wallow motionless except when yawning. Our dock isn't far from the graveyard which offers a small but very choice selection. The names are etched in white stone, on calm days we pay our respects to Sir Ernest Shackleton with a champagne toast. The diesel tanks are lined up as neatly as the graves—a reminder of how much blubber was processed in this cove. Inside the factory humans once dismembered whales, now time is dismantling the factory. Silence weighs on the dilapidated halls, the skuas fly in other skies. The whale oil tanks still exude a stench, so it seems to me: it's hard to breathe in the middle of the rusting slaughter-works. Here and there a roof slants downward between the clouds and the tin floor, red signs mark off an area infested with asbestos. In front of the bone-rendering plant three figures clamp their hands around an iron chain and lean back as though in a tug-of-war with long dead whalers. The wind carries a sound of giggling, the Filipinos enjoy playing hide-and-seek in the ruins. But how am I supposed to distance myself from this flensing deck, this place synonymous with death? The snow-covered mountains are mere backdrops, distant and detached. So well hidden are the fur seals that you have to pay close attention not to step on one by accident. The younger seals scamper into the water, twisting in mid-dive, then give themselves a vigorous shake as soon as they crawl ashore. A stand of gentoo penguins keeps watch between an anchor and some ship's propellers (which, uncoupled from their purpose, are nothing more than grotesque jetsam), mocking glances behind red beaks. And by the jetty the *Albatros* has listed ostenta-tiously for decades, its harpoon gun long turned landward.

"Hello hello, hey it's our guide, what an interesting

place, isn't it; just like you say, this is where humans and the Antarctic got to know each other, it sure is quite a mess, they really ought to clean it up, do you know what that building was for?"

"There are some plaques on the other side, along the main path, with detailed information."

"You're not going to make us traipse through all that mud now are you, Mr. Zeno, now that we've run into you."

"That was the blubber cookery, Mrs. Morgenthau. First they carved the whales up here right where we are standing, then they extracted oil from the blubber in giant cookers."

"That sounds like hard work."

"Lucrative work. With high returns. In a good year they cooked away up to forty thousand whales."

I politely take my leave, otherwise I'd have to explain how first the fur seals were skinned, until there weren't any fur seals left, after that the elephant seals were killed for their blubber and the try-pots were heated with penguins when the fuel ran out, and when there weren't any elephant seals left the penguins were rendered into oil. Everything was put to use—humans are always so eager to show Nature more efficient ways to manage her resources. I tramp across a gently sloping soccer field: the crooked goalposts a comforting sight. Slaughter by morning and soccer in the afternoon. Did the goalie's hands stink? Were the striker's shins streaked with blood? I leave because I know what they would say, the same thing everyone is always telling me: How come you have to be so negative? Why do you always insist on ruining the mood? Can't you leave off just for once? The same thing over and over, burbling around me from dawn to dusk: don't take it all so seriously, relax, stop picking on everything, turn a blind eye, things won't work out so bad, nothing's as awful as it seems—everyone has installed the same software: deflect, downplay, be ready to duck when the storm hits. I wonder what words would have sprung to their happy lips if they'd been hauled off to the clinic at Pentecost, just as summer was settling in, with a persistent pain in the chest. A whole week of examinations. Probes boring into my body, as though the pain had to be hauled up from the deep. And then I spent days waiting for the life-saving operation and after that three months recuperating. When the doctors declared I was (almost) fully recovered, I dropped my bag at home and dashed off to the glacier, leaving Helene staring dumbly behind me.

The mere sight of the strangers in my compartment got on my nerves. The woman sitting opposite—my equal in age and disappointment—was holding a box of chocolates. She cautiously untied the ribbon, removed the marbled paper cover and carefully laid it on the seat to her left, then positioned her fingers over the selected confection like the grippers of a crane and lifted it from the box with clinical precision. The candy quickly disappeared between her pale-purple lips, with hardly any sign of chewing as she closed the box and retied the ribbon, only to tug at it a few minutes later and repeat the entire pedantic operation. No matter how many pieces she removed, the outside looked completely untouched, as though the candies were intended as a present. At the rate she was going she'd have nothing but an empty box with a fancy bow by the time she got to Kufstein or Klagenfurt. Meanwhile the man sitting by the window was using newspapers—first *Bild* and then *Krone*—to shield himself against the swelling landscape. He gave the appearance of wealth, a middle-class man ready for first-class travel on that hot summer day, faint marks on his suitcase showed it had once been covered with tacky tourist decals, perhaps he'd acquired some aesthetic guidance since sticking them on. The man studied the first tabloid from top to bottom and then proceeded to the next with similar dedication. Such keen regard for sensational headlines and pathetic ads irritated me. I had to step out into the corridor. When we reached Salzburg three girls with blank faces entered our compartment, without paying any attention to us old-timers. The woman permitted herself another candy, the man remained buried in the *Krone*, the three girls regaled one another with gossip from school, and when the train stopped in the middle of a field I was overcome with the fear of being trapped in this compartment, my view blocked by the *Krone*, with nothing to eat but a last piece of candy, my ears ringing with the vapid talk of the young generation, and never being able to make it back to my glacier. The train started up again, I calmed down somewhat, little did I know things would only get worse. So I wouldn't have to wait for the bus in my weakened condition, the host of the Zum Kogl guest house picked me up at the station. A shaggy dog was panting in the back of his jeep. I have to tell you right away, you're not going to like it, something's happened, you're not going to like it. The road was all switchbacks and hairpin turns, with bare landscapes on both sides: without ice and snow the Alps are grossly ugly. I'm glad to see you're back in shape, we prayed for you, our whole family—the man has seven daughters, or is it eight, in any case all daughters, and praying isn't alien to him. For a moment I was distracted by a racing cyclist hurtling downhill, the car swerved left, the wheels grated on the gravel, I looked up through the windshield and saw . . . nothing. No glacier. No living glacier. Only fragments, individual pieces, as though its body had been mangled by a bomb. The escarpment was still iced over, but all that was left further down were lumps of darkened ice, strewn over the cliff like rubble waiting to be removed from a building site. All life had melted away. I told you it would be hard, that's not a pretty sight. The host's voice evaporates in my memory. Apparently I climbed out of his car without saying a word—so he informed me that evening over beer and *Tafelspitz*—and staggered from one shard of ice to the other, as though drunk or blind, reminding my host of the farmers saying good-bye to their livestock during the Mad Cow scare, so he told me that evening. I wasn't capable of such a gesture, I was too stunned, all thoughts and feelings paralyzed. I knelt next to one of the remnants, the ice under the sooty-black layer of dust was clean, I ran my fingers across the cold surface, then across my cheek, the way I always did, performing my ritual greeting. In the past I could plunge my arms into the fresh

snow and bring up full scoops that made my hands so
cold they would revitalize my face. I licked my index
finger, it tasted like nothing. Only then did the first trivial
thought occur to me: never again would I be able to fill
plastic bottles with glacier water to sip so enjoyably at
home. My host was standing next to his vehicle, I
brusquely signaled for him to leave me alone. Then I lay
down on the scree, all balled up, a picture of misery, I
would have welcomed any emotion that didn't hit me
like a positive lab test result. Not knowing what else to
do, I stayed like that until a hiker put his hand on my
shoulder to check on my condition. I snapped at him.

"You're hiking here?"

"It's amazing up here, isn't it, and such a beautiful late
summer day."

"Don't you see what's happened?"

"Oh well, not much snow this year."

"This glacier is dead, and you go sauntering blithely
past. Get lost, disappear, you disgust me."

The man didn't deign to look at me again and went on
with his hike. It would have been pointless to calculate
the volume of melt for this September, to take the balance
of the summer. There was nothing left to measure, not
on this mountain. At some point I got back on my feet
and climbed uphill, heading no place in particular. On
the steeper terrain a stump of ice had survived in the
shadow of a desk-sized rock, it served as a temporary
support, I set down my notebook, the wind leafed through
the pages. What hadn't we measured and weighed? And
what of all the findings we had compiled, the models we

had constructed, the warnings we had issued in careful scientific format? The pages of futility are filled with noble ambitions, they need to be torn out, every last one, our methods have failed us utterly.

We had issued warnings, but in vain, things only worsened with every passing year. Only when it is too late do people hear Cassandra's voice: today even more sanguine souls have joined the chorus of doomsayers. Nevertheless I hadn't foreseen this degree of destruction, not when the snout disappeared (I had just turned fifty), not when the tongue broke off and the calved ice melted away as quickly as it did (I had just turned sixty), and now this blow from the blind spot of our calculated optimism. If even the experts are surprised by the terrible speed of the demise, whose intervention can still save anything, whose point of view matters, since everyone else harkens to the rotten call of comfort and convenience? My work had consisted in documenting our delinquency—the father confessor masquerading as a scientist.

I pounded my fists on the stone table, in my pain I thought of the girls on the train, chewing with difficulty on the gum of life, these three girls who pass in the world as innocent. But what is that kind of innocence worth, when we all know they're bound to wind up guilty? That is what lies ahead for them as well as for us, they will continue this devastation, they will go on destroying the very foundation of life. They don't give a damn, just like most of us, they won't rest until they've consumed polluted squandered destroyed everything. I left the following morning. In the next valley over, the surviving ice surfaces had been shrouded with white burlap, under which an emaciated glacier was emitting its death rattle. I felt like a doctor in a hospice.

We called it "swimming"—swimming in the river of ice. When we dared drop into the moulins, the glacier mills, to use them as chutes, trusting ourselves to the twists and coils as if the glacier were obliged to protect us as we slid on the seat of our pants through pipes of the purest blue. It was dangerous, moderately dangerous, we had checked to see where and how we would emerge, even if we occasionally miscalculated the acceleration and came shooting out of the shaft like a cannonball while it thundered underneath, so that even the person who was brushing the pain off his pants had to laugh at the glacier's acoustic commentary. Yes we gathered our share of bruises, but we really got to know the glacier, we stuck our nose in every crevasse, we even believed we could hear the icy creature sliding into the valley on a layer of its own water, and we were amazed at the multi-hued splendor within what seemed to be a monochrome universe. We opened our eyes (and not just under the polarizing microscope) to its delicate spectrum, the colors in the flatland seemed garish by contrast. Where the ice was as hard as alabaster we found blue caves which we decided to enter right then and there, afraid we might not be able to find them again when we returned. Afterwards we went our separate ways, some hurried back to the city, others retreated to the valley, in the end I was the only one who chose to shuttle between glacier and university, on solitary days I abandoned myself to the tranquility of the ice, the clang of the water, I became a stone pressing on the ice and leaving my own imprint, and one time I was surprised to feel the urge to pray inside one of the icy cavelets that served as my makeshift chapel — not to God (and how vain a deity to command his name be held so sacrosanct) but to variety and abundance (written out like that the words seem wooden, and it isn't enough to replace "God" with "Gaia" either). All alone I searched for insight within the clearest and coldest blue, I filled the icy caves with my own variations of the eternal, just like the monks of long ago who filled their stony grottos with drawings, only why didn't they see the stone itself as a perfect image of God, the weathered surface, the patches of moisture? *Deum verum de Deo vero*, can truth reside in such a phrase? Within my blue chamber, in the belly of my frosty whale, God has dispensed of every superfluous word.

Jeremy is small and rather nondescript, but his glasses make him instantly recognizable wherever he goes, they look like they were lifted from some California comic strip that transforms every polar expedition into a heroic saga, especially those of Ernest Shackleton, whom Jeremy worships above all others, he can give his lecture on Shackleton six times in one season, each one fresher and more original than the last. If they're not on duty other lecturers will lurk near the door to the auditorium so they can listen for at least a few minutes as Jeremy hoists Sir

Ernest to promethean heights (if our Californian whiz kid were looking for spiritual role models he would undoubtedly place Shackleton alongside Isaiah and Jeremiah). He's seen me writing in my notebook with its heavyweight cover, I don't try to hide this activity, it's impossible to keep something like that secret, and anyone who believes otherwise will soon be disabused of the notion, because on board ship everything can be seen and anything seen can also be heard. Jeremy surprised me by placing a handwritten note under the service plate, which I manage to read sometime between hors d'oeuvres and dessert: "Since I see that you, too, are keeping a journal, I feel you should take a moment to remember Nathaniel Hawthorne, who once applied to join Charles Wilkes' US Exploring Expedition as official historian. His hopes were thwarted, however, after a certain Congressman opposed to his appointment argued that 'the style in which this gentleman writes is too wordy and ornate to convey a genuine, sensible impression of the atmosphere on the expedition. Furthermore a man so talented and cultivated as the said Mr. Hawthorne will never be able to grasp the national and military significance of any discoveries it may make.' I found this tidbit in my readings. You should feel fortunate to have free rein to do what your colleague was prevented from doing, even though like him you will probably never be able to grasp the national and military significance of the Antarctic. Therefore: eschew prolixity and stylistic embellishment, and think upon Shackleton and the deprivations he endured." When I looked up I saw that Jeremy was once again pointing his camcorder at me, I held the paper in front of my chest like a kidnapped hostage, and swore the just-invented Shackleton Oath to uphold the Unadorned Word. Jeremy grinned and panned out away from me through the glass and onto the ocean. He would be welcome on any expedition because his good mood is infectious even when he is pensive. That is a rare talent. Of course he can hardly help summoning old Shackleton, every one of us identifies with the man (all but El Albatros, that is, who can't get over the fact that Shackleton planned to sell albatross chicks to gourmets in London and New York, his hunger had made them particularly tasty), he is the Good Man of Antarctica, the famous photo of *Endurance* trapped in the ice is on display in the elevator, and the explorer's portrait is hanging on the wall in front of the dining room, he could easily be a member of our group, he'd get along well with us, he mistrusted strict hierarchies and valued communality over subordination. Above all he was the only polar explorer who traveled to the southernmost part of the planet knowing it would likely be his final destination. He could no more imagine a grave in thawed ground than he could everyday life in moderate temperatures.

Having taken our time in Grytviken the captain calls for full speed, the *Hansen* plows through the swells, water water everywhere, as though we were the first sailors to pass through this sea. Barely three hours off of South Georgia we see whales, very close. Beate is so excited, when the humpbacks dive she holds her breath, and inhales together with them when they resurface. Her enthusiasm is undiminished by the dozens of cameras clicking and snapping around her like whips, did you see them, she calls out to Jeremy, who has blazed a trail through the dense spectatorship, and who calls back, "Oh yes, I did, I see we're already clicking into place, too."

••• — — — •••

He'll have to hell to pay that's for sure, I've also kissed some French girls, what kind of crazy choreography is that, who come from Paree. All told we're talking about 220 passengers, English, Germans, Americans, Dutch, Swiss. Oh, you must have taken a wrong turn at the big intersection, now you'll have to go back the whole way. Norwegians, Brazilians, Canadians, New Zealanders, Austrians. We know enough but we understand little, the last spasms, not the faintest idea, to cum in the mouth costs double, the conditions there are unimaginably extreme, it's snowing pornflakes, we're infesting now in our future. Go ahead Foxtrot Two Niner, over. I can see people, dozens of them, standing in little groups, over. Have you tried to establish contact, over. Yes, a few are waving their arms, over. What is their condition, over. I can't tell, over. Any signs of panic, over. No signs of panic. One group is very close together, it looks like they've formed a chain, over. No, cows aren't holy, sheep goats and cattle aren't holy and wild animals aren't holy either, nor are the birds of the sky or the fish in the sea, pigs aren't holy and neither are chickens, not even the lamb is holy. Foxtrot Two Niner Foxtrot Two Niner, go ahead, over. They've formed a circle, over. A circle? over. Something like a big zero, over. Descend as you can and fly a few 360s to calm the people, over. Wilco. Out. The experts are disputing this prognosis, today the fixed price for lithium was announced on time, thrushes are dropping dead from the sky, and so this planet Earth spins around its own axis and never stops moving. Email the passenger manifest, on top of that there are 78 crew members, we have to find out as much as we can about the experts on board, we'll look for every missing person BREAKING NEWS RESCUE OPERATION IN EFFECT BREAKING NEWS RESCUE OPERATION IN EFFECT nothing else matters

••• — — •••

7.

60°11′5″ S, 50°30′2″ W

WHENEVER I WAKE up early I run sixty laps around the weather deck at a fast pace in the sleepy gray light. I'm wide awake, the waters of the Antarctic are running alongside me, flowing around me, clockwise, accompanying me on my laps just like Hölbl did decades ago when we circled the sacred temples of Ladakh early in the morning, before the workday began. It just seemed like the right thing to do, although some people accused us of trying to ingratiate ourselves with the locals—people eager to dismiss sincere interest in broadening horizons as some kind of smarmy xenophilia. Hölbl dubbed the venerable Lama "Maestro Boltzmann" and His Holiness took a mischievous pleasure in the nickname, sensing that the unfamiliar sounds contained a certain prestige, and he wasn't wrong. The water creaks and groans, the waves are only a few meters high, our crossing is relatively calm, the Drake Passage is usually good for at least one storm before letting a ship into the eye of the hurricane, into the paradisiacal tranquility of Terra Nullius. I perform my rotations in sync with the Circumpolar Current that every moment spins one hundred fifty million tons of water, birds glide through the twilight, their sharp wings slice through the cold air as they loop through the sky in perfect figure-eights, white albatrosses soar in steep arcs, storm petrels dive like rash decisions and disappear behind glimmering crests, plunging into the feed troughs between the waves, and I circle on, with each of my steps the ship recedes into oblivion right under my feet. I would be perfectly content with this solitary round dance of self-forgetting and nothing more if duty wasn't calling: I have another lecture coming up in just a little while and I have yet to update the announcements about our upcoming landings. Every day at 7:30 PM I can be found at the radio coordinating plans with the other expedition leaders. Some of the voices I recognize right away, and some have accents that leave no doubt as to their countries of origin (Beate claims this is entirely natural, even whale songs show regional differences, underwater dialects). At the moment there are eight ships in the vicinity of the Antarctic Peninsula, just among ourselves we divvy up the mooring places that were booked months earlier, we trade sites and help each other out to make up for cancellations due to weather. And we stay out of each other's way, after all we don't want the sight of another ship to ruin the illusion that we're all on our own here in the Antarctic, far removed from any regulated traffic, alone at the end of the world.

No one in the institute had any illusion that I might consider changing my object of inquiry (the very phrase makes me think of an ingrown toenail), not at an age when my beard is straggling toward retirement. Nonetheless I couldn't continue as I was, the Alps had become unbearable, what was there to be gained by accompanying one more glacier to its death? And to go on giving lectures undeterred seemed as grotesque as teaching veterinary medicine to paleontologists. No, there was no alternative but to bow out. Two colleagues invited me to join them in the High Caucasus Mountains. They didn't want to see me leave the institute, and for that most sentimental of all reasons: they were used to my being there. You can cook for us in base camp, they joked. Actually I was considered an exceptionally gifted chef, a reputation that rested solely on the large pot of Jamaican fish tea soup I always brought to our summer parties. The first time I made it they were all dumbfounded, no one expected a dish like that (with that name, those ingredients, that taste) from me, a man who considers the tropics anathema in general, the Caribbean a steam pit in particular, and the idea of serving frutti di mare in the foothills of the Alps the epitome of decadence. And I would have no idea about the soup if a certain Jamaican who grew up in England hadn't fallen in love with a young woman from Munich. He made ends meet teaching advanced conversational English at the Münchener Volkshochschule, where we discussed ska lyrics by Madness and read excerpts from George Mikes' *How to Be an Alien*. At the end of the semester he invited the whole class over, gathered us in his kitchen, and then with the flourish of a circus director he opened the lid of a pot with a diameter as big as an oak's and let out aromas that could spawn legends, fantasies of lazy afternoons rocking on boats with straw roofs or of diving into scallop beds. I took the course again the following year, even though my English was in good shape—not least thanks to an intensive exchange with colleagues from the University of East Anglia and the Jawaharlal Nehru University—just to get another taste of this soup and some idea how to make it. The recipe is incredibly elaborate, this Jamaican Fish Tea contains all the treasures of the sea, the ingredients are difficult to obtain (requiring the combined forces of the Viktualienmarkt, Dallmayr and Käfer), the preparation has to be planned well in advance and started at least one day before the feast. I spent weeks looking forward to this day, a day that knocked on my door with a tattooed hand. In the Caucasus, though, I'm not exactly in my culinary element, as I told my colleagues, and besides I can no longer bear the sight of living glaciers. That was a lie and they knew it, I still loved ice, but my perspective had changed, when I used to look at a glacier I saw history and change, abundance and endurance, the face I now encountered was grotesque, the remaining ice had become a mirror of our own neglect. From here on out no matter what I might see, I would never be able to recover my earlier acceptance of things. It seemed to me as though only now did I perceive their essence. Behind all the cornices and all the stucco I saw nothing but prisons. The people crowding the shops in the pedestrian zone struck me as display mannequins, pushed and pulled hither and yon by random jerks and jolts. You don't need someone like me on your team, I said, and no one contradicted. That year saw the last pot of my Jamaican fish tea soup.

On a ship at sea it's hard to get out of the way, the passageways are straight and narrow, it's best to stop and turn so you're back is against the wall, pull in your stomach and don a broad smile that makes it easy for the other person to glide past. Everyone on board is quickly located: within a few days it's clear who has set down roots where, which binoculared guest has staked out which spot in the hope it will content him throughout the trip, an armchair in the crow's nest of the Panorama Lounge, for instance, where it's easiest to escape the ones who can't keep still, who change positions every fifteen minutes, heading now to the weather deck now to starboard now to port because they're afraid of missing something, who soak up every scenic view and then rush back inside where it's warm, on to the next lecture, the next film, to coffee or afternoon tea. And those who have paid a great deal of money for a top-of-the-line suite may under no circumstances be disappointed. Emma at the reception desk tells me that no one can teach the art of complaining as well as rich people. As Expedition Leader I am fair game for the restlessly inquisitive, passing from Deck 3 to Deck 6 is like running a gauntlet of questions. I prefer sitting in the bistro, where every second table has a jigsaw puzzle — postcard scenes, carved into 500 tiny pieces waiting to be put back together so as to match the picture on the box, and whoever succeeds can graduate to 1,000 or 1,500 pieces, clearly all puzzle-piecers must be happy people. I sit down at one of the tables for two, across from Mary, who keeps her recording device running even while she sketches away in her unlined notebook with a sharpened pencil, the Antarctic Ocean is on my left, and on my right is Paulina, who plays the part of the indifferent waitress with furtive joy, repeating my order with intense concentration, as though it were the first time she'd heard me ask for a double espresso with a good dose of foamed milk, but foam only please, so as not to drown the taste of the coffee in a lot of milk, she recommends the marble cake which I detest, whereupon Mary orders a slice just out of solidarity. We have just crossed the 60th parallel, I explain, only now are we truly in the Antarctic, from this point on ships aren't allowed to dump waste water, which naturally limits the length of our stay in these latitudes, an additional advantage of this sensible regulation, after all this is the only ocean humans still haven't polluted, and that's the way it ought to remain. Just four percent, says Mary, while I take a swallow of water, the Antarctic Ocean makes up only four percent of the Earth's surface water. Outside, a flock of cape petrels floats past on invisible pillows of air. Paulina serves the coffee and cake with an air of professional efficiency and practiced nonchalance. Mary thanks her by name, which she reads off the tag pinned over Paulina's breast pocket. Paulina responds with an exaggerated smile before turning to me and asking, "Anything else, sir?" Whereupon I answer stiffly,

"No that will be all, Paulina, thank you." Mary asks what I think would happen if it weren't for the Antarctic treaty. "There'd be a public discussion about the exploitation of the Antarctic and lots of bargaining behind the scenes. Lobbyists would stress the need for mining and oil exploration, and a campaign would be launched against the penguins with the slogan 'Should we give up flying just because these birds don't know how?' The penguins would no longer be photographed standing up but lying down, so that they looked plump and a bit dodgy, as though they were begging to be slaughtered. We can give up the luxury of our sentimentality at any moment, and there's no guarantee this won't happen prematurely, despite the treaty, when the going gets tough, who'll pay attention to voluntary obligations when even binding treaties don't count for much."

"A whole lot of people would have to exert pressure to keep that from happening." Mary interrupts me with a naïve enthusiasm that does my heart good and hurts at the same time, my face betrays my skepticism. I might excuse her remark, thinking how weighed down I must seem, perhaps, she says, it's because I lack the experience of a common struggle that would give me courage, I would like to forgive her, but she really shouldn't say that. I yearn to feel euphoric. We go on talking about ice and the world, she asks questions that require answers beyond the usual prepared platitudes, and all of a sudden I hear myself confessing how I sometimes feel ashamed to be working on this ship, especially on this trip when I'm even more responsible because I'm Expedition Leader, the tourists should be sent elsewhere, to a theme park, to a traveling Capsule of Eternal Ice that can be set up anywhere, you enter through the front and leave by the back, but I myself couldn't live without my sojourns in the ice, and she looks at me so full of understanding that I tell her about my theory of mass hyperthermic cognitive dysfunction, a syndrome with symptoms that mirror those of hypothermia when overexposure to cold addles the mind to the point that people freezing to death suddenly feel warm and start taking off their clothes. This paradoxical undressing is known as hypothermic cognitive dysfunction, and sets in when the body temperature drops below 90°. And while we have scientific proof that people in this state lose their ability to think and therefore to save themselves, I don't know of a corresponding temperature threshold marking the onset of the hyperthermic equivalent. But it's obvious that our collective mind is similarly addled, since we keep turning up the temperature on a planet that's already unbearably hot. Mary seems bewildered, suddenly she's avoiding my eyes—does she consider my theory stupidly silly or simply smug?—she stares off to the side, or have I alienated her in some way? The way you trumpet out your so-called convictions, Helene once snarled at me while we were fighting, makes them sound like insults. Mary doesn't react to my soothing chatter, her gaze is paralyzed, focused on a point at the other end of the room. Her face goes blank, surely it's not my fault, and it's hard to imagine that the sight of the small, husky man stretched out in one of the armchairs and fingering a book and staring off dreamily might have hijacked her attention like that. "Mary, what's the matter?" Her face has broken out in splotches of red. It takes a while before she answers me. "That man, what's he doing here, what does he want?" Before I can ask another question she has stood up and scurried off, leaving her paperback and recorder in my care.

My sadness scabbed over into rage. The semester hadn't yet begun, it was easy to avoid running into people. Helene pounced on every invitation and stayed out of the house as long as she possibly could, assiduously representing the two of us, she even drove out to her mother's by herself to celebrate a round-numbered birthday, I don't know if she concocted something about a present being from the two of us. How long might it have gone on until everyone simply forgot she was actually part of a couple? Whoever believes in constancy and steadfastness must despair at the rapidity with which individuals couple and their unions break apart. At first acquaintance, the other person is an impregnable fortress, three dates later, after a few kisses and some mediocre sex which both sides sugarcoat, all drawbridges are let down. The lie of eternal love attunes us to the lie of eternal life. Later we have a hard time explaining what the fuss was all about. During my first weeks alone I conducted an experiment on myself, with curtains drawn and lights dimmed I sat on the floor and resolved not to get up until I had recalled half a dozen sexual delights in exact detail—something more substantial than the faded memory of a breeze wafting across our bodies or velvet-soft skin. But even after hours of

biographical excavation I couldn't do it. Instead, my brain
called forth athletic achievements as vainly as I had stored
them: three times in a night (in the ski lodge, as a student),
two hours without stopping (to win a bet with Helene
when she claimed I didn't have the stamina). At some
point I had to get up and get groceries. Every acquaintance I came across inquired with urgent concern about
my convalescence. I disappointed them all. Instead of
sharing some uplifting tale of my narrow escape from
death, I told them about a glacier that had been exterminated, and that annoyed the good souls, they walked away
shaking their heads and rendered disparaging judgments
before they even reached their cars and drove down dead-
straight streets into their remotely controlled garages and
from there quietly ascended in paneled elevators up to
their wallpapered crypts. They considered me ungrateful,
either toward God or fate or the health system. "Well well,
here I thought we'd lost you but I see you're still alive and
kicking," the vegetable peddler pontificates—the same
man who charges a lot more money for just a little more
taste. It's uncanny how orderly everything is in Solln, and
how resolutely the Blessed defend their idyll with all
myopic means. My neighbor pesters me with an account
of his illness, as if we owed each other some reciprocal
sympathy. "Just because our pain is similar doesn't mean
our suffering's the same," I told him, and that was the end
of his pestering concern. What a happy circumstance that
people quick to interfere are so quick to be insulted.
Unfortunately this kind of self-disclosure wasn't an
isolated case, lingering illnesses were being tooted and

touted on every channel and frequency, as if contracting
a severe disease were the most remarkable individual
achievement of our era. You have cancer, how extraordi-
nary, prostate or breast or lung or liver, you have ulcers,
how exceptional, your body is wasting away, oh my, it's
being consumed from within, how astounding. The
sunniest beaches are littered with melanomas, this obses-
sion with one's own miniscule existence is nothing more
than pitiful, what bloody fucking miserable bastards.
"Hey, I understand that," Paulina interrupts my jotting.
"German's a lot like English, isn't it?"— because those
last words I've just written in English. Paulina loves looking over my shoulder (like she's doing now) and especially
loves it when she recognizes what I'm writing, even if it's
some crude obscenity like that. I hardly notice the English
words sprinkled in, here it's rare that we native speakers of
German are all to ourselves, so my German is becoming
anglicized step by step. To prevent me from suffering the
same fate as my first expedition leader, who jumbled
English and German into a kind of gobbledygook, and to
keep my own language crystal clear, I often retreat to the
weather deck and mumble poems to myself that I learned
in my youth, poems our teacher Herr Stradel assigned us
in the Frühlings Gymnasium, which we wound up learn-
ing by heart (in my case on my way back from school),
without a clue that they would stay with us forever.

Das Gestern, das mich flieht, kann ich nicht halten,
Das Heute drückt mich wie ein Frauenschuh.
Die kleinen Wandervögel schon entfalten

Die Flügel herbstlich ihrer Heimat zu.
Ich steige auf den Turm, die Arme weit zu dehnen,
Und fülle meinen Becher nur mit Tränen.

"Translate it for me," Paulina requests as she so often
does when she looks at a page I have filled with my scribbling. If I translate that into English it won't make much
sense, I say, pushing back my chair, but if I translate it
into Paulinish we'll both understand it better. My hands
have taken hold of her wrists, my lips caress her neck,
she pulls back and retreats to the bed. "Every word has
at least two possible meanings," I mumble, a left-handed
clumsy meaning, my mouth sucks hard, and an always-
has-to-be right meaning, my mouth leaves one nipple
and wanders to the other, slowly crossing the hollow
between her breasts, the tip of my tongue drumming
against her skin.

"I'd like to come inside you without you noticing."

"You say the craziest things." And here it is again, this
laugh, the most lovable thing about *Homo sapiens*, and I
say: "Yes." More than that would be too much chatter, her
laugh turns to moaning, we are sinking, air bubbles rise to
the surface of the water, we are sinking, everyday colors
vanish from sight, we tarry in the deep as if we could hold
our breath as long as we wanted. When we surface I listen
with one ear to the latest rumors which she stirs up the
way a gust of wind blows a raked pile of dried leaves (it's a
feast for the ears when she and Esmeralda fill the refrig-
erators every morning. Their mouths rattle away like
sewing machines, snatches of overheard conversations

are immediately reworked into colorful elaborations, while the bottles clink and clink as they're taken out of the boxes and loaded side by side.) At the beginning of our relationship I was worried that her liaison with me might damage her esteem in the eyes of her fellow Filipinos, but in fact the opposite happened, when it comes to cruise ships in the deep southern latitudes I'm evidently considered a good catch. I open the curtains, the expedition leader is entitled to a good view, Paulina was used to windowless sleep—the only thing that's the same in all the rooms is the screens.

> And now there came both mist and snow,
> And it grew wondrous cold:
> And ice, mast-high, came floating by,
> As green as emerald.

Paulina maintains that German sounds beautiful, she doesn't learn any vocabulary, she catches useless words such as *Waschlappen, Hauruck, Kasperltheater* (which in her rendition has limited recognition value) and inserts them into the least appropriate situations. I'm sitting undressed on the edge of the bed, looking at half of myself in the mirror that's mounted on the bathroom door. The years have not simply passed, they've folded themselves into my skin, deposited themselves on my hip, and there's no reason to assume the invisible half might show anything more reassuring, it's a mystery to me how Paulina manages to ignore everything that by rights should dampen her desire. Instead she leans forward and her lips touch my scrunched-up penis with the lightness of a scarf grazing the skin.

Fog is setting in, it's not rising off the sea but hovering above it, just enough to let the light safely in its lock before passing it to another level. Now the iceberg behind is discernible only by its base. A bird slips out of the mist and flutters past. "And a good south wind sprung up behind; / the Albatross did follow." "We humans have eyes made for hunting," says Jeremy, "our nose could fall off without great loss to our senses, our ears serve only to uglify our face, but our eyes are sharp and alert, they can be relied upon." "Especially," I add, "when they fix on something in order to kill it."

••• — — •••

Get a move on, bigmouth, no I'm afraid we don't have any hotels here, no guest rooms either, you know we never get visitors unless they've lost their way. The *Urd* is already in position and has begun rescuing the passengers, but it can't take everyone so the rest will have to be divided among the other ships. Get a move on, trackdog, don't lose that scent, estimated arrival is in forty-five minutes, the Spanish girls are lovely, rent-a-friend, oh yes indeed they are, a friend for rent, cut. As soon as we heard the sound of the motors someone suggested we should form the SOS again, as a warning sign, with us on the ice and not a ship in sight. Pipe down, 24 percent of those polled believe that nature has its own right to exist, but the ladies of Calcutta, blackbirds are dropping dead from the sky, cut. We had already begun to disperse, although the lecturers kept trying to herd us back together, we probably could have managed to make a smaller SOS, everyone immediately wanted to make the O. Cut, two cotton candies and two carousel rides for the price of one ginger-bread heart, first the saplings burn, then the shrubby underbrush, the young trees, the dead wood, and all that just fans the fire, the price never reveals the truth. We formed the O very quickly, it was way too big given our numbers, someone called out, come on over here, let's make the S, I could hear people screaming in other languages, cut. Don't give up, go hog-wild, cool off, best put your hopes on ice, cut. I hurried over to help out with the S, thinking surely we can pull that off, in any case it was a lot smaller than the O, and that was it, we didn't get any further, cut. The wildfire reaches the flashpoint and consumes the tallest trees, it blazes away, hotter and stronger than ever, starlings are dropping dead from the sky, are sweeter by far, then comes the third fire that burns everything away, destroying all life, the third fire is the inferno that burns down the world once and for all, cut BREAKING NEWS STRANDED PASSENGERS RESCUED FROM ICE BREAKING NEWS STRANDED PASSENGERS RESCUED FROM ICE all ablaze

••• — — •••

8.

62°12′9″S, 58°56′43″W

ON MY FIRST trip to the farthest south I emailed Father a few photos — "penguins & son," "frosty morning mood," "sea meets sky," "land of ocean" — using the address of the director of the assisted living home, with the request she show them to him on her computer. His reaction was predictably gruff: how disappointing you didn't just vanish into the unknown. If this Internet business can stretch its tentacles that far then there's no place left on the planet where a person can really be alone. I should have thought twice before clicking send, given Father's general outlook. When he looks beyond the horizon he's not longing to find Atlantis, he doesn't dream of crossing the desert to Timbuktu or discovering Shangri-La — all he wants is the peace and quiet of a solitary hike. He couldn't possibly understand why I get antsy if I miss my routine fix on the website of the European Space Agency (by way of the WLAN connection on Deck 4) where I track the breakup of the Antarctic Ice Shelf. I know it's proceeding at a pretty fast clip, so why do I have to keep verifying the fact? I still haven't told my father anything about King George Island, otherwise his notion of the virgin icescape would be trampled on by boots both moon and military. Even as Expedition Leader I can't keep us from landing here, we couldn't put in at Elephant Island because of wind speeds exceeding 56 miles per hour, so we don't have any other option. King George Island is 90 percent ice, 10 percent research stations and penguin colonies, that's how I would have to describe it to him, the stations are a few decades old, the colonies have been here for 30,000 years. The island counts as a spearhead of human settlement because it houses the only hotel in the Antarctic, the Estrella Polar (except the hotel has closed down and Polaris can't possibly be seen from these latitudes), as well as a military outpost for the Chilean Air Force, which can also be used as a jumping-on point by impatient ecotourists who contrive to bypass the Drake Passage. The landscape is infested with research stations. Every country that wants a say in the future of the Antarctic, I would explain to Father, has to maintain a permanent station, and the most economic place to do that is King George Island. Russia, China, Korea, Poland, Brazil, Uruguay, Argentina and Germany are all vying for the Antarctic Cup. The bases are close together, which would hardly seem to foster any sense of scientific rigor, while at the same time feeding the suspicion there's more rummy than research

going on, that people are just biding their time waiting
for the day they're allowed to drill for oil and not just
ice (at present all truly groundbreaking research is
being conducted deep in the ocean or far inland,
during the summer the field teams are always on the
go, camping out on the ice). Every now and then we
visit Chile's Eduardo Frei Station. The sight of the
settlement rising from the shore, the makeshift buildings—bank, post office, store, school and hospital—
delights the passengers, it's practically a normal village,
there are women and children, it flies the national flag,
issues its own stamps, and sends newly minted Chilean
citizens into the world who with every cry for their
mother's breast advance their country's claim to the
Antarctic peninsula. How is it possible that neither the
Soviets nor the Americans have launched a highly
pregnant woman into space just so she could give birth
to the first extraorbital baby and thereby establish a
legitimate claim to the solar system, the galaxy and the
universe itself? I would tell Father that we're avoiding
the Russian station Bellinghausen on account of the
many derelict oil drums, the wreckage and scrap iron
that litter the shore, exposing the true legacy of the
human race: rusty garbage. But there's also a colony of
chinstrap penguins, we put in close to that, the calls of
the black-and-white-uniformed animals merge with
that of the red-uniformed humans into a kind of high-
pitched cacophony as the extraterrestrials land,
equipped with curiosity but lacking a common tongue.
But the chinstraps may be more used to such

intrusions than we think, as El Albatros explains, between the launch of one Zodiac and the arrival of another: evidently they're equally unable to communicate with the gentoo penguins who stray into their colony, it's not even certain the chinstraps notice the interlopers. But the passengers do notice the natives, they savor every minute they are allotted with the penguins, we have to insist loudly and urgently when it's time to go back. As the passengers come ashore I stand with one leg in the water next to a metal stepstool that allows them to take hold of my arm and land on relatively dry ground while I mumble polite mantras — even if after two hours in the freezing water I'm ready to chase off every Antarctic tourist with a savage grimace and a primal scream. A stream of phosphorescence streaks through the water, I steady the Zodiac, a spritely Swede climbs in and shows me his drawing of a penguin with its beak pointed skyward, a few strokes, the barest approximation, a large inflatable assault craft rushes past full of soldiers, the Chilean flag painted on the side of the bow, it comes dangerously close before veering away, leaving a wake that causes me to lose my grip on the dinghy, and then makes land not far from us, right in the middle of a large flock of penguins who reluctantly waddle apart. The first soldier jumps off and immediately lights a cigarette. He takes a few steps inland and stands right in the middle of the colony, his posture relaxed, a cigarette dangling from his mouth. Our passengers, whom we have diligently schooled to keep the proper distance and the appropriate demeanor, stare in disbelief. "Take over," I say to Jeremy and set off in the direction of the soldier. "Wait a minute," says Jeremy. "What are you doing?" I call out. The soldier looks at me blankly. I point to his cigarette, and with unmistakable gestures demand that he stop smoking. He ignores me completely, turns to his comrades and smirks, this look-at-me smirk that makes me turn white with rage, I start screaming bits of Spanish, I run up to him, shouting at him to stop, and grab him by the arm. With a single unexpectedly violent motion he shakes me off, I tumble a few steps, then try to lunge at him but fall clumsily to the ground, my face lands in the mud. He takes his pistol out of the holster, releases the safety and points it at me. Suddenly Beate and El Albatros are at my side, they both try to reason with the soldier, in Spanish, they hoist me to my feet and hold me firmly between them, as if they wanted to prove to the soldier what little threat I pose, I stare at the man, shaking, he looks at me with disdain and turns away. El Albatros holds me tight while Beate distracts the passengers who have quickly surrounded us, forming a colony of humans. I stand there without moving for some time, and finally El Albatros decides it's ok to let go of me. The soldiers have turned their backs to us, they are already marching off, no one can say where to or to what purpose, a few wisps of smoke curl into the air, and I wonder where those cigarettes will be ground beneath their boots. Only now does my body feel the fear and at the same time I am euphoric, a lump rises in my throat and simultaneously disappears.

My penumbral life began in the autumn following an excruciatingly hot summer. How easy it is to call everything into question once you start. The longer I stared at my surroundings the less sense they made. The blanket of rationalization we knit for ourselves—which is billed day in and day out as the ultimate truth—is easy to undo once you get hold of a loose end. One jerk and suddenly all flaws are exposed, revealing a jumble of competing realities: a global summit, delegates dozing off in the plenary session while hostesses in outlandish costumes pass up and down the aisles, popping candies (or maybe pills?) into the open mouths of the participants, who munch away in their sleep. And when their mouths reopen they rise one by one and sleepwalk to the podium, where they regurgitate the same pablum, which at the end of the day is collected and served to a patiently waiting press, which reports on achievable policy goals and the best possible deal under the circumstances. These are not living breathing beings so much as middlemen of destruction. It doesn't go down well with the Comfortable & Contented when you shamelessly insist on unraveling the yarn. The louder I voiced my opposition, the more stubbornly I was ignored, little by little the neighbors stopped inviting me to their beloved grill parties. Cheers! The keg's just been tapped and we're in complete agreement, everybody gives a lot and doesn't take much, we're all easy-going and eco-friendly, let's not get bent out of shape, despite everything life's pretty bearable. If I contradicted, Helene would give me a chiding glance from where she was sitting with her lady friends, who acknowledged my existence the same way a mechanic might regard a car headed for the scrapyard. I knew she was only waiting for the suitable occasion to slam the door behind her. As the time we spent together shortened to weekends only (and not many of those, as my field trips alternated favorably with her bridge tournaments) we had less need to put up with each other; it was a pain to be locked up all day and all week with her in the same house. You have to get help, she told me one day, I don't know what's with you, but you're losing it. That made me furious. She had hurled the first stone.

"I hate to be the one to tell you this but you took out the wrong insurance, and that was a pretty stupid thing to do"—I had picked up one of her special dishes—"because we don't really need fire insurance or flood insurance. What we do need is a policy to protect us from a madman on the loose in our own house, a man on the verge of losing it at any second, and we need it now and we need it desperately too bad you didn't take out that kind of insurance, what a shame"—at that point the Gmundner deer bounded into the wall and burst into pieces—"uh-oh that's what it looks like when the madman goes berserk"—here some pieces of Delft majolica smashed into a window with a great *fortissimo*—"who knows what's next, nothing's safe anymore"—and I banged my open palms against the china cabinet with all her porcelain treasures, a decorative bowl slid off and fell on my shoulder before shattering on the floor—"did you think I'd simply put up with everything? Didn't you think I realized how you've been trying to force me into your Procrustean bed? Do you think I'm some kind of

fairground steer waiting for my fellow humans to guess
how much I weigh?"

"Fellow humans?" Helene interrupted after a grating
scream, "What fellow humans? You no longer have any
fellow humans."

Here I fell silent. I had been weighing the Portuguese
rooster in my right hand but I set it back down and
concentrated on taking a deep breath. If she was right and
I really had lost my mind then we'd no longer know if I
was sick or if I had found freedom and release. We fled to
the TV to avoid further interaction and stared at the
screen with fierce tenacity, following nature shows the
way a hunter tracks a wounded animal, we sat silently on
two armchairs while a mutual contempt stretched out on
the big brown sofa between us, consuming everything
that had once united us, back when we were all we
needed, on clear nights under a handful of stars. Nothing
could placate me, every digitally reproduced animal
struck me as a captured creature that was first castrated
and then skinned. And so we suffered through evening
after evening until some foreign station broadcast that
wondrous news bulletin about masses of snow plunging
into a valley, even though he wasn't live at the scene of
the catastrophe the reporter's voice quivered opera-like
with fear, so stunned he could only stammer, while I
perked up wide awake and leaned forward in my seat and
started rooting for the majestic avalanche. "Down the hill
down the hill!" I shouted, and then with renewed courage
and strength, "Into the valley into the valley!" and when
the snow swallowed the first house so quickly the

structure didn't even have time to collapse I shouted, "Show no mercy show no mercy!" Then it rolled over a second house, and a third one, an entire farmstead, I cheered out loud when the entire village vanished into the snow, and the anchorman was reduced to silence for several seconds until a technical glitch was solved and the white surface vanished from the screen. Helene stood up and walked out of the room, ostentatiously shaking her head. A few days later a letter from her lawyer put an end to our television evenings. I dumped our TV in the bin for hazardous waste: broadcasts that sublime were far too rare an occurrence.

Back on board ship no one looks at me directly but everyone does so behind my back, as though I were dripping with foolishness—humiliating events like that quickly make the rounds. Mary might understand why I behaved the way I did, but she is nowhere to be seen (she was with the first party that landed early that morning, she had greeted me briefly before hurrying ashore). For lunch all I have is soup so I can retreat as quickly as possible. Even Ricardo refuses to give me his usual welcoming grin. The lecturers at the table eye me with concern, no one reproaches me for my lack of self-control, even though each would have dealt with the situation better, they are more than lenient, perhaps because they would regret having to do without me. Beate gently asserts that we can't make a crooked world straight, Jeremy tells about the time a military transport vehicle ran him off a road in the Rocky Mountains. He's just illustrating how he drove his rickety pickup into a spruce tree when I stand up, nod curtly and leave the dining room, avoiding every sideways glance. There's nothing in the cabin to attract my attention. I'm lying down on the bed, staring at the fire alarm when Paulina bursts in, a breathless bundle of nerves.

"What happened?"

"You've already heard?"

"You got into a fight with one of the passengers?"

"With a soldier. It wasn't a fight."

"Soldier, what kind of soldier?"

"A Chilean."

"How so? What did he do to you?"

"He was smoking right in the middle of the penguins."

"What do you expect from a soldier?"

"Not to smoke."

"The people who join the army aren't usually the brightest."

"It's not a question of intelligence."

"What is it then?"

"It's a question of respect."

"And you get into a fight over that?"

"It wasn't a fight. He didn't stop smoking when I told him too."

"He didn't listen to you, that's what it is, you always expect everyone to listen to whatever you say."

"It's not about listening to me but to their own common sense."

"And now?"

"I don't know."

"You do something like that and you don't know what's going to happen next?"

"That's right."

"You're pretty dumb, you know."

"Agreed."

"You're putting us at risk is what you're doing, and what for? For nothing."

I would defend myself if I could find the words to match the anger I felt when I ran up to the smoking smirking soldier and he stood there shrugging his shoulders. Everything I can think of is after the fact, flowers on the grave. Paulina is sitting on the bed across from me. My silence proves her right. With my hand on her shoulder I draw her to me, her hair touches my chest. She buries her face in my shirt. I feel the cloth getting wet. The day will come when I will make her unhappy without being able to console her. A first kiss, a pause for thinking, a second kiss. We take off only what we have to and I push inside her, over and over, with throbbing futility. We are silent, stirred and embarrassed at once because we are misusing our bodies. I feel impatience welling within me, I want to finish as quickly as possible. I hear Emma's voice calling my name over the PA system. I am being summoned. Someone wants to ask me an urgent question. I have to go back to work, says Paulina. We are both pent-up. I come with pinched lips.

A few years ago, two summers before the catastrophe, Helene and I went to Lisbon for a long weekend, another attempt to salvage our marriage with sightseeing, late dinners by dim light and mutual smearing of sunscreen. We strolled along the avenues and climbed the steep narrow streets, taking advantage of every delight Lisbon has to offer, venturing into alleys unmarked in any guide, we savored warm pastéis de Belém at the bakery of the same name (touristy, very touristy, but when I am a tourist I appreciate what is staged for tourists), drank Alentejo wine, admired azulejo tiles, and even boarded a catamaran to watch dolphins in the Tagus Estuary. But no matter what we encountered, nothing moved us both at the same time. We could have spent days in the souvenir shops without finding anything that would have the same appeal for the two of us. We stumbled into a church that had earned a mere three lines in the tour guide, fully expecting to step back out after a fleeting glance at ceiling and nave, so we wouldn't have to spend too long in a place where we were the only people. But I found myself mesmerized by the interior, by its imperfection, the signs of destruction sparked in me an unhoped-for feeling of devotion, for the first time inside a house of worship I felt I was in a real space and not simply a temple to human megalomania. Traces of the fire were still visible on the columns, a blood-orange vault stretched out overhead like a broad sky above a battlefield. In this *igreja* the promise of salvation carried a credible patina of soot. The wilting flowers and flickering candles seemed like last vain hopes. It took me a few minutes to notice a pillow-soft song wafting from some narrow loudspeakers, children's voices that seemed to come from the other side of a wall that can never be surmounted. In a small apsis I saw the most moving Virgin Mother I had ever seen, all alone in a gapingly empty niche. She radiated an air of uncertainty, as though she were afraid of not being able to satisfy all the petitions presented to her. She was an injured soul who had been driven out of her home. I felt her pain. Not only because her son had been tortured to death, but because her torment had been immortalized. I studied her a long time. "And can you tell me what it was about that dilapidated church you found so fascinating?" a grumpy Helene asked when we were outside the portal. I said that the church should really be called the *Igreja de Gaia*—a sanctuary one visits to cast aside all human hubris.

Dan Quentin is aboard the *Hansen.* He never moves without an entourage, which is why his presence cannot be discerned but only deduced from all the blowflies swarming around him. Now and then his tousled mop of hair can be seen drifting by. His manager offered me the prospect of an audience, he didn't use the word "audience" but his tone of voice and choice of words suggested some form of homage. The excitement on board ship is palpable, the passengers are in high spirits ever since I called them together—in two sections according to language, first English and then German—and announced they would have a historic opportunity to play an active part in a work of art. I described the necessary safety training, Quentin's manager outlined the basic artistic plan. To my amazement the passengers did not feel at all bothered by the slogan "Art needs you," in fact they felt flattered and discovered their inner activists. "If I'm being called on to do something for the environment then count me in," a businessman from St. Louis declared, setting the tone for the others. "The young man has imagination and that's exactly what we need," acknowledged an elderly lady, "instead of all those protests all the time, they do nothing but undermine the cause." "I'm assuming our participation is worth at least a signed photograph," a retired high school principal from Paderborn demanded. "Naturally each of you will receive a signed copy," the manager reassured them, "and what's more every single one of you will be listed by name on our website. And if you'd like a limited edition print for someone you left back home—and what a gift that would be, right— naturally you would qualify for our special participant rate, which is quite generous." The passengers left the room in little groups, chatting away, to go sign the lists that had been set out for those who chose to take part. Finally there was only one person left, a haggard, unshaven man with a black woolen cap, who had boarded at the same time as Dan Quentin. He had spent the winter at the Arctowski Polish Antarctic Station and was now on his way home after nearly twelve months on King George Island. He was sitting in the next to last row, one chair away from the passageway, his hands resting on his thighs, fingers splayed, a smile pressed on his lips. He fixed his eyes on me, evidently expecting a reaction. I sat down beside him, still holding the microphone.

"I should speak about wintering over."

"You'd like to give a lecture?"

"Everyone wants to know what it's like to spend the winter in the Antarctic."

"Like being in a tunnel, right? That's how I've heard people describe it, except at least you know exactly how long the tunnel will be."

He grabbed the microphone from my hand and shouted into it, "That's false!" Then he let the microphone drop to the floor. "You have no idea how long the tunnel is. With every passing day you start to doubt more and more whether the sun's ever going to come back up, whether you'll ever be able to move about freely again, whether you'll see more of the world than a few floodlit measuring instruments, whether the tunnel has an end at all."

I picked up the microphone and turned the red switch to off. Live mics usually lead to embarrassing situations.

"You'd go crazy if it weren't for the books. Are you surprised? Such a banal idea, books in a tunnel. Did you know that Amundsen took three thousand?"

"Should we sit down over a cup of tea?"

Trusting in the saving power of imagination while stuck in a seemingly endless tunnel made sense to me. I accompanied the Pole to the coffee machine, which also dispensed hot water. He went on talking while he awkwardly unpacked a tea bag.

"Science has become our modern oracle, I sensed that early on, but it wasn't until I was in the tunnel that I really understood"—he dumped several spoonfuls of sugar into his mint tea. "It used to be that knowledge was gained with the help of a medium. And meanwhile we assumed we were well beyond that, we dismissed soothsaying and prophecy as hocus-pocus, we were convinced that we could complete our calculations and our future would be revealed, that we would provide sober proof,"—the Pole tapped his spoon on the edge of his cup—"evidence obtained through precise research, that's the sign of our time, the blueprint for future behavior. All we have to do to convince people is show them the appropriate data. Isn't that right?"

He turned around, still holding his cup, looked up and down the stairs, looked up and down, stopped, lifted the cup to his lips with both hands and slurped his tea.

"And who did they first worship in Delphi? The goddess Gaia. Her priestesses would sink into an ethylene-induced trance in order to look into the future. So what about us? We produce vast quantities of ethylene, it's everywhere, in our clothes, in everyday objects, it's even in our bodies. We're all on narcotics, we're all so addled by this drug of consumerism that we've lost any and all clairvoyant ability."

The Antarctic overwinterer took another slurp. He was standing just inches away and speaking from his heart, but a real conversation seemed impossible.

"Have we even asked ourselves who should we turn to now? What oracle should we consult? Some higher instance, that much is clear, but which? The one we call Nature? Gaia? Maybe even God? Have our questions become any more precise? Perhaps. Do they lead to new answers? We assume so. And we were so certain that the more we figured out the better we would act. Ridiculous. And you, what are you doing on this ship?"

It took a moment to realize he was talking to me because he was still facing away, and his voice hadn't changed at all, the words kept limping at the end of every sentence like a bad leg.

"Have we veered off track? Just a little bit? Very much? False, once again, false. We've completely missed the mark, we've been playing the wrong hand, we were holding onto our projections and meanwhile it turns out that prophecies were trumps. The projections proved as irrelevant as last week's weather forecast. Admit it, you didn't think it possible that they'd simply cast a deaf ear to all your warnings."

"How do you know that?"

"You told me yourself."

"We've never met before."

"You explained it all to me in great detail."

"Where was that?"

"At some congress."

"I don't remember."

"So you turned away from science? You gave up?"

"On the contrary, I'm just planning to give my next warning in a different way."

We are hemmed in by sameness, we sense that nature is staring at us blindly but that is all. The water has a greasy sheen, a little ways from the ship the surface forms an opaque screen separating two metallic visual horizons. All cameras have been lowered, the lounge is quieter than usual. Paulina and I exchange glances above the glass display stand with the marble cake. When we reunite I plead with my own desire, desperately searching for some sign of favor. Gradually we come to a standstill as we rock back and forth on a false promise.

••• — — •••

You can't really say that, the ladies of Calcutta, why didn't you fill up at the last station, didn't you see the sign, no more gas for 500 miles, you mean you miscalculated? That was very rash of you, I can't give you any gasoline, here's a bottle of water, I can't do any more to help. Will steal your heart away, at present we can only confirm that Zeno H. was the perpetrator, but we still don't know whether he was acting alone or with accomplices, we can only speculate about his motives. The older the better, when I kissed you and called you sweetheart, if you're still feeling fine have some more wine, do the chairs in your parlor seem empty and bare. We don't know anything about his whereabouts, he waited until the helicopter was gone, then he took the captain, the first officer and the security officer prisoner, a command sounded in the engine room: all hands on deck, what's going on? Get up here quickly. Do you gaze at the doorstep and picture me there, when does MILF turn to GILF? When the money runs out we'll slaughter a billionaire, oh-kaaay, the rich are the piggy bank of the nation, oh-yessss. One day he stormed outside and started screaming like a holy terror, it was impossible to tell what he was saying, he was completely unintelligible, the neighbors opened their windows. Is there anything else you can add? It wasn't a normal scream, it gave people the shivers, you could tell, and deep down inside I was terribly afraid. When we have to choose between preserving nature or earning money, trip the trannies in a trap, it could be worse, robins are dropping dead from the sky, the troop's all poop, you can't really say that, ciao ciao bambino, Robotnik gets it on with Futanari, we like to grope in the dark, twiddle twaddle, it's easy to remember, Shotacon is stalagmite, Lolicon is stalactite BREAKING NEWS FATE OF HANSEN STILL UNKNOWN BREAKING NEWS FATE OF HANSEN STILL UNKNOWN now it's time to roll up your sleeves again

●●● ━ ━ ●●●

9.

62°58′9″S, 60°33′6″W

If we were pirates—and we're not, we're privateers with letters of marque that we call standard form contracts, we no longer slit throats, these days we do our murdering with unmanned drones—this would be our hiding place. If we were in a pirate film we would put in at our secret island on just a day like today. The ocean is slate gray, the sky ash gray, our ship is sailing straight into a closed mass of anthracite-colored cliffs, if "open sesame" turns out to be the wrong password we'll get smashed to pieces, the captain has throttled back the engines, we are barely making headway, as though a hobbyist were tweezing us through the neck of a bottle. Everyone is crowding onto the weather deck with their binoculars, scanning for a solution to the riddle. The secret passage appears, the hidden opening which sailors of old called Neptune's Bellows. "Do you want to go in the water?" Paulina had asked before we fell asleep. Of course I do. The basalt cliffs are perilously close, rigid and unyielding, like frozen fury, it's easy to see where the volcano left its mark, the flow lines from the lava. Ahead is a black sandy beach covered with lapilli and divided by half-sunken ruins, behind that a rise shadowed with snow-caps, the rocky cliffs in between are glossy black and flecked with oxidized iron. Our ship drops anchor in the middle of a caldera. Even here humans established themselves, and soon the volcanic bay ran red due to the rising demand for baleen, used at the time as corset boning, and for whale oil, which went into nitroglycerin so people could blow each other up in the trenches of World War I. What wondrous innovation to make explosives out of whales, what a vibrant symbol of progress: destroying the essential to create the superfluous. Decades later, the volcano took belated revenge, singeing away all human presence. Deception Island is a demanding port of call, we all have our hands full, not only do we ferry the passengers ashore, we also take everyone medically fit on a longish hike. We used to dig a pit in the sand so the Antarctic tourists could bathe in the sulfurous warm water, but that's no longer allowed, now the passengers have to jump into the ice-cold sea (and jump out quickly if they want to survive, the Brazilian doctor stands by with stopwatch in hand, making sure no one stays in longer than forty-five seconds). Afterwards we distribute certificates testifying that they took the plunge. When the doctor goes back on board I jump in, the last to do so, and let myself be revived by the icy water.

As soon as you've finished your second spell in the sauna you have to go in the cold water, Hölbl instructed, and I mean really in the water, a cold shower just won't do it. Even though I always loathed saunas I followed his recommendation, because the near-naked ladies were lounging on the barstools and if you spend too long ogling you get depressed. Well, is it just as I promised or not? Didn't I tell you I'd take care of you? Patronizing as he was—he even insisted on helping me tie my bathrobe—thanks to Hölbl I got to know the institution of the bordello and its fleeting encounters. I also appreciated some things he hadn't mentioned, such as the matter-of-fact parting from the woman I had just thrust myself into scarcely half an hour earlier with a simple "see you around," before her backside disappeared around the corner and out of my memory, superseded by others swaying past, and the happy, relaxed exhaustion that settled inside me as the sediment of a new experience. After a few more visits, some even without Hölbl, I managed to dispense with any preliminary conversation at all, it seemed inappropriately binding. In the club he introduced me to, which we frequented during the interregnum between divorce and Antarctic because of its favorable value-for-money ratio, there was a small "cinema" with a "playground" instead of chairs or sofas, where the clients could relax, naked but for a towel wrapped around the loins, and watch a ridiculously bad porno film, or if they were so inclined, the uninhibited goings-on around them. Now and then an unclothed woman would stroll past with an affected "Would you like a little company, honey?" To my ears that sounded like a threat, which is why I only accepted more original solicitations. Apart from such siren calls the encounters were entirely to my liking, reduced as they were to the bare minimum. Without a word I would motion for her to remove my towel and start to work. As if I were sitting high on a Ferris wheel, looking down at the life below, in miniature, with no idea how I was supposed to return to Earth. Now and then I managed to avoid the exchange of invented names, those were the happiest occasions, my bodily needs were satisfied and the whole process had nothing to do with me.

Before the ship passed through the narrow opening, the captain took me to task, abandoning his usual terse style. On the bridge, in the presence of several stakeholders (as they were known in the language of the hierarchy), he reminded me that as Expedition Leader I was expected to set an example, if I take a wrong turn so does the entire ship, my highest priority is the security of the passengers, a man my age ought to be able to control himself, one cigarette isn't going to incinerate the entire Antarctic continent, I had endangered the collaboration with the Chilean station, damaged the reputation of the cruise line, at that point I stopped listening, who is the captain to be judging my fit of rage. It's true that the following day I felt a sense of disgrace, but I also still felt I was in the right, the soldier had violated the agreement allowing us to be in the Antarctic in the first place. My only regret was not having made a more forceful impression on him. I stared past the captain's head through the curved window and out over the sea toward the icy horizon to see the soldier flicking his cigarette into the middle of the penguins, the butt landing on the thick mass of feathers, singeing the shimmery blue-black, it's not the first cigarette, either, the penguins are in the middle of an enormous ashtray that's never been emptied, even though they cannot fly they spread their stumpy wings, trying to escape. When I come back to Earth I hear the captain informing me he is going to report that I am poorly suited for the post of Expedition Leader, unfortunately he finds himself compelled to reexamine my continued employment as a lecturer, and this may require a psychological evaluation. Then without any transition or words of regret he immediately moves on to Dan Quentin's SOS project, which since seems to have garnered both his approval and his appreciation. That's nothing but a lot of ballyhoo, I say, the captain's tongue-lashing having freed me from any diplomatic constraints. He tells me to make sure everything comes off smoothly, so that I can have an honorable departure.

"And what exactly do you expect to gain from it?" I ask. "Are you gunning to get invited onto a talk show?"

"That kind of effrontery doesn't become you."

"It's not effrontery, it's just being upfront. Setting up an SOS like that without cause is ridiculous. You're letting yourself be used as his stooge."

The captain tells me to stop acting so self-important and see to it that this work of art happens, nobody attaches any importance to my outlandish opinions. I tell him that this work of art can't possibly succeed unless there's a genuine emergency, unless the SOS formed by the passengers is for real, now that would be a success, can you imagine how well the photos would sell then? He tells me to stick my outburst somewhere else and take care of my job, one preparedness maneuver, one hour, one photo, a high point at the end of a beautiful trip, that's not all that difficult, and afterwards we'll take everybody home and that will be the end of it. The captain has nothing more to say to me, the stakeholders' stare at me like I'm a freak in a carnival sideshow.

The pianist has been watching me as well, but he doesn't speak his mind in front of the others, certainly not in front of the woman from New Zealand who is traveling with her aged mother and who longs to be noticed on her own, sans parent. Ever since the previous evening he's been eager to oblige, perhaps a bit too hastily, but the New Zealander doesn't seem like someone bold enough to insist on the proper tempo. She asks me if it's true we can send postcards from Port Lockroy, which I confirm, and immediately take the opportunity to tell her a little about this British outpost, an old whaling station later retooled for purposes of espionage, because the British were afraid German ships might hide in the many natural harbors along the Antarctic peninsula. The plan was called Operation Tabarin, a scheme so secret even Churchill didn't find out until it was already in progress, the seamen sent to guard the Bransfield Strait waited and watched and waited and watched for days, weeks, years, but the Germans never showed, they'd probably forgotten all about the Antarctic, being otherwise engaged, so the soldiers manning the post had nothing else to do for the rest of the war except chow down on duff pudding and

lick Lyle's Golden Syrup off their spoons. So the enter-
prise was entirely in vain, the New Zealand mother asks
somewhat simplistically. Not entirely, they did manage to
remove the Argentine flag from Deception Island. The
pianist interrupts to say that as always, whenever his
esteemed friend the Expedition Leader explains something, he only tells half the story, what he failed to mention
was that in 1939 the Nazis had flown seaplanes over the
Antarctic and dropped flags rigged on metal spikes in an
effort to reclaim part of Queen Maud Land for Germany.
And when they had staked the area with their swastikas
they renamed it New Swabia. The woman from New
Zealand seems delighted, either by the twists of history or
the studied charm of the piano player, she smiles demurely
and repeats New Swabia as if it were a punch line.
Meanwhile, behind me at the bar others are waxing witty
and inflicting their humor on Erman, listen you'll love
this one, my first name is John and my last name is Walker,
so it's John Walker and what do you think they call me,
Johnnie, right! So go ahead and pour old Johnnie Walker
a Johnnie Walker and I guess that means it has to be a
double, there's no two ways about it. Why did it get so
gloomy today around noon, a different voice asks, from up
by the bow it looked like we were sailing into the land of
the dead, then another voice breaks in, ahoy, ahoy, we're
the Pirates of the Antarctic, followed by hoots and hollers,
I turn to see the faces flushing red with laughter, the
constant hullabaloo through which Erman's calm voice
passes like a silver thread, Black Label, sir? Naturally,
keep it coming, fill up the old skull . . . and crossbones

please snorts Mr. John Walker, Erman makes a face, presumably in reaction to the spittle, just wait, you'll stop hooting soon enough, the New Zealand mother–daughter leaves, the bar pirates grab their glasses and stumble out. Now the pianist can say what's on his mind. He hadn't expected that of me, what childishness, picking a fight with an armed soldier over a cigarette, I better start using my head and learn to pick my battles. He absolutely understands my aversion to cigarettes, for his part he has a hard time summoning sympathy for the passengers, what's there to like about Mr. Johnnie Walker? The cigarette was yesterday, tomorrow we have Dan Quentin, that's even worse, despite what happened the captain still wants me to organize this SOS business. Well as the only certified doomsayer on board I have no choice but to accept my fate, there's little he could contribute unless we need some musical underscoring. He gets up and moves to his keyboard, titti tatta tam, titti tatta tam, titti tatta tatta tam, a memorable synthesizer intro for someone who was married to Helene longer than the band ABBA existed. His choice is dead on, too—the Johnnie Walkers of pop music. Fits Quentin like a glove. But SOS stands for another song, can I guess, he plays the first notes, I recognize it right away, hello darkness my old friend, come on, sing along, he plays the whole first verse. You know what I was haranguing the captain about? I told him there'd have to be a genuine emergency to make the whole thing believable. That's the spirit, how about a hijacking? The scenic cruise goes Crusoe. He laughs, and his laughter is clear and refreshing, like a spot of sorbet

between heavy courses, then it morphs into an impro-
vised variation on the refrain from "The Sound of
Silence." He tossed out the idea so casually, just like that,
a tiny nugget in the quarry of mindless remarks that make
up our conversations. A hijacking? A red SOS on the ice?
The moment when art becomes reality. The idea takes
hold of me and doesn't let go. Even the most casual utter-
ance can be taken seriously. What starts as a hairline frac-
ture widens into a crack and finishes as shattered glass.

A white bird alights on my head, the glacier hides behind
its threshold, it calves into the ocean, loud, alive, seagulls
flutter above the glacier and disappear, the clouds are
tiny, a wave rears up and crashes, spewing spray from the
crest high into the air to form a lacy burial shroud, albatrosses plunge from the sky like falling rocks, while blind
hope gets caught in the mounting mesh of mist.

•• — — •••

Let us dream beneath golden stars, this is a dead end, you
don't seem to want to understand, in this neighborhood
there are nothing but dead ends, secret dreams beneath
green trees. At gunpoint (and where did he get the pistol?)
he forced all those still aboard the *Hansen* including the
captain into a life boat, then he set off, yes these days
steering a cruise ship is as easy as moving a joystick, there's
no doubt he's reached open sea by now. Let us dance to
mandolins, we are all as innocent as the subsidies we
receive, now the stage is bare, dance beneath golden stars.

Would you please tell us your name? Paulina Rizal. And your occupation? Waitress on the MS *Hansen*. How long have you known Zeno Hintermeier? Four years. How were you acquainted? We were friends. What kind of friends? Just friends, not accomplices. Were you in a relationship with him? No, we hadn't promised ourselves anything. Did he mention what he was planning to do? No. He didn't warn you? He talked a lot, they were just words, nothing but words. I'm sorry for coming so late, my appointment lasted longer than anticipated, no, I missed it, what did you say? Yes, no, no, I'm listening, I was only distracted for a moment, there's a white pigeon fluttering around here. He's headed straight north, the fighter pilots can't attack the ship, they can only observe it, it will have to be boarded, there's no other solution. There's hope for you yet, little gifts can do a lot to nudge a friendship along, come take me by the hand and lead me off to fairyland. He was a buzzkill, a nutcase, but at least one with convictions. You wouldn't understand him. Don't underestimate us. You wouldn't understand him, you'd have to change completely in order to understand him. In the past everything had to be stored, stay tuned for our flirt tip of the week, at times the glacial surface calls to mind a coral reef, and so it goes without a pause BREAKING NEWS PHANTOM SHIP REACHES THE ATLANTIC BREAKING NEWS PHANTOM SHIP REACHES THE ATLANTIC and now for something completely different

··· —— ···

10.

62°35′0″S, 59°56′30″W

IT'S TRUE, Mrs. Morgenthau's mishap could have been prevented if I'd been less negligent, if skuas didn't swipe penguin eggs, if I hadn't suggested we put in at Half Moon Island, a crooked stretch of land shaped like a crescent moon, with four evenly distributed hills and masses of chinstrap penguins, in good weather an easy jaunt, with a glorious view of the Livingston Island peaks, a small strip of terra firma perfectly suited to my taste, overwhelmingly white with a few black stony patches, in one place a forked cliff of granite next to an inclined rhombus, a formation I never tire of looking at, and even if the weather was changeable during the day, there was no compelling reason to forego the landing, on the contrary, the capricious light seeping through the heavy black clouds made the island seem as if it had been fashioned in some fit of euphoria. Despite our advice the passengers seldom manage to stay in one place so they can actually observe the animals, preferring instead to run around and follow the penguins every which way across the snow, cameras at the ready, with the praiseworthy exception of Mrs. Morgenthau, who stood at the edge of the colony keeping the prescribed distance and watched enraptured as a mother or father penguin warmed their eggs, "The second egg really is smaller" I heard her mumble, like many of the passengers Mrs. Morgenthau enjoyed comparing what she'd learned in the lecture with the reality (in the words of our ornithologist El Albatros: the second egg is really just a backup, that's why it's smaller, just like an emergency parachute is smaller). If she'd been less attentive, less reverent, she wouldn't have felt such a kinship with the brooding penguins and would not have intervened in this idyll, whose peace was disturbed only by skuas hunting for eggs, an instinctual behavior I hardly noticed anymore, in contrast to Mrs. Morgenthau, who had fixed her attentive gaze on an especially aggressive raptor, an ugly, fat, mean bird, as she told me later, she felt a palpable aversion to the skua and was getting all worked up, it had even frightened her a little, as laughable as this sounds it's the truth, that explains what happened next. All this might have been avoided if I had reacted more quickly, if I'd been more focused, if a different guide had taken the easy post near the chinstrap penguin colony at the fateful hour, instead of myself, who, tired after a few hours manning the landing area, had declared a break and was consequently ill prepared for the skua's nosedive, which I only glimpsed out of the corner of my eye when I heard Mrs. Morgenthau cry out,

"It has an egg," just in time to see the bird land less than three steps away from her, a white egg clutched in its talons. I saw the skua look around for any threats before attempting to crack the shell with its beak, which it never managed to do, because Mrs. Morgenthau fell upon the bird and snatched the egg with a surprisingly nimble movement, then held it carefully in her hands while the defeated bird flew away, leaving her proud of her rescue, if also a little puzzled, as was I, which is why I didn't react immediately, but only after she'd started heading toward the robbed penguin, who refused to move because it had to protect its second and now only egg. Mrs. Morgenthau reached its nest with the best of intentions, bearing the egg like an offering, bowing before the bird so she could place it as gently as possible in front of the penguin's abdomen, all I managed was a hasty "Don't do that!" but in vain, Mrs. Morgenthau felt that she had been chosen to right a wrong, that she had been called to return the egg with future life unscathed to the brooding penguin, an intention that was as noble as it was misguided, because the penguin, faced with an attacking red monstrosity, driven by instinct to protect its remaining egg, opened its beak and bit Mrs. Morgenthau in the left hand, causing her to drop the egg as she screamed in horror and stared at her hand as blood went dripping onto the stone, an amazing amount, I don't know if she ever felt me grab her arm to check the wound, because she tore away to escape the snapping penguin, then slipped at the first step and went crashing into another penguin, who was guarding eggs of its own and as a result couldn't get out of the way quickly enough, just as I didn't react quickly enough to stop her fall, and the helpless bird was buried under Mrs. Morgenthau's massive upper body, the penguins caught on sooner than I did, the entire colony squawked and squealed into motion as I helped Mrs. Morgenthau up, her parka smeared with bits of egg, I steadied her with one hand and used the other to radio El Albatros before examining her wound—the penguin had bitten deep into the soft flesh between her thumb and forefinger — things wouldn't have been half so bad if I'd cleaned it right away and prevented an infection, but my backpack was missing the first-aid kit we were always supposed to carry, so that I had no other choice but to staunch the wound with my handkerchief. Below us lay the lifeless penguin, while a harsh chorus of protest erupted from all sides, I was about to suggest we make our way to the dock when a few snow-flakes landed on our hands, I looked up, the weather had shifted, a blizzard was coming on, the wind started howling, visibility was decreasing at a breathless pace, the bridge let us know that in view of the rising katabatic wind, which could easily overturn a boat the size of a Zodiac, it was advisable to stay put on the island, and if necessary pitch the emergency tent and take shelter until the gale had passed and the ship's horn gave one long and three short blasts. El Albatros showed up as shot-sized hail began to fall and then the storm swallowed everything: peak and glacier, the four hills and the forked granite cliff, the other guides and passengers and even the penguins, now the doctor couldn't possibly reach us, Mrs. Morgenthau was at the mercy of Half Moon Island, El

Albatros inspected her hand and my blood-soaked hand-kerchief, visibly worried even before he whispered to me using his broken German to keep the diagnosis secret from the patient, the wound had to be disinfected with all urgency, penguins' beaks are heavily contaminated, the bacteria are highly dangerous for humans (the doctor later told me that because of the extreme conditions, Antarctic viruses and bacteria are extremely resistant), he himself had rushed over without a backpack, since I hadn't told him I needed a first-aid kit, which is why the doctor is completely right when he says it all could have been prevented, the fact that Mrs. Morgenthau wound up bedridden in the hospital ward on an IV drip, with a fever and a swollen hand, most likely a case of erysipelas, which used to be known as "holy fire," the only thing certain is that it was a good hour before we managed to bring Mrs. Morgenthau, clearly in shock, and the other passengers on board—leaving behind a dead chinstrap penguin, a few crushed eggs, and a skua who was robbed right out of his beak.

The move from the house in Solln to a furnished one-room apartment in Moosbach was very different than the previous relocation. Everything I still chose to call my own fit in Hölbl's VW SportWagen. The only books I took were ones I had practically learned by heart during the past few years, the rest wound up in the recycling bin, I went there every day for weeks lugging two heavy canvas shopping bags, one in each hand, the CDs had to be taken to a special station for used electronics that was a longer walk, but they weren't as heavy. On my way I remembered what Lama Boltzmann had told us about a library in a Tibetan monastery with scrolls that no .one had been allowed to inspect for hundreds of years. The priests would look at the stacked documents and make prognostications about the future. In light of this tradition my trip to the used electronic collection point struck me as a kind of Buddhist pilgrimage: we need texts that remain unread on purpose, music that is intentionally not listened to, trees mountaintops brooks glaciers that are deliberately left in peace. As the summer dragged on I spent my days reading in the Moosach apartment with a sense of liberation, freed from the besetting pressure of thousands of books. My only concern was what to do with the proceeds from the sale of the house, a substantial sum even after I had transferred half to Helene. Once again I abandoned myself to the tried-and-true texts, inspired by their stubborn ambition to appeal to my conscience, which is presumably why they continue to be so esteemed, even though they try as hard as they can to change the way people think. The classics are allowed to shine light into the darkness and fashion words worthy of chiseling into stone facades. Living authors, on the other hand—so I discovered each time I opened the newspaper—are expected to have more modest aims, to motivate here or agitate there, but under no circumstances should they propose to change the world. So how are people expected to stir things up during their lifetime? Shaming doesn't work, because everyone is ready to publicly confess their disgraceful deeds, pathos doesn't work because everything is downplayed. And violence? Violence is the only language that has yet to be plastered with the ads and logos of sponsors. Left to our own devices, we understand only the violence directed against us: violence done to others remains incomprehensible, unheard, voiceless — nothing more than a rasping cough in a throat without speech, or at best a stutter. That's the kind of sentence I penned in the margins as I bided my time in my cozily narrow apartment in Moosach, reading my own notes and asking myself whether I had found a reasonable response to the unreasonable demands of our time, or if I, too, had been infected by the idiocy of the age. One thing seemed clear, though, namely that true liberation can only succeed through a creative act. Occasionally I wrote emails. Even in the dreariest weeks I made sure to keep up my correspondence with a handful of colleagues I really respected, for instance Shiva Ramkrishna from the JNU in Delhi, who took a devilish delight in interpreting the latest scientific findings through the prism of early Sanskrit myths, in his opinion the melting of glaciers and the impending threat of the Ganges running dry had been foreseen, the ancient prophecies foretold that the holy river would one day grow tired of the countless sins that had been washed away in its waters and would disappear below the earth, even our gods will change, Shiva wrote in his latest email, you can get a taste of things to come on the Siachen Glacier, where the soldiers are so completely dependent on helicopters for food and protection that they are inclined to see them as omnipotent saviors, their only hope for deliverance from the mind-addling tour of duty 20,000 feet above sea level, and have even begun to worship the machines, with gyrating light and ancient chants that they have only had to adapt slightly. Why shouldn't God be a helicopter, I answered Shiva, that would say something for the range of religious imagination, Christianity's biggest mistake was fashioning God in man's own image. Once a week I interrupt my musings to talk to Paulina over Skype, at a prearranged time. I don't appreciate surprise phone calls, not from Hölbl, who absolutely refuses to understand that the recollection of Paulina is far more erotically satisfying than the sight of some scantily clad long-legged female from one of the shantylands newly accepted into the European Union, nor from my bank advisor (the title says it all, the man advises his bank at the cost of his client), who has tried to fob off everything imaginable on me including the lousiest bonds and securities (and what a phony word that is, right up there with "insurance"). But his efforts are in vain, he still hasn't grasped that he's at a complete disadvantage since I don't need to convert my time into money. Sometimes I'm so annoyed I simply hang up. I stay away from the Alps, I don't venture out of town, either for little outings nearby or longer excursions farther away—there isn't any nature left in my country, I might as well let myself be moved by the cultural landscapes printed between two book covers.

Glacier fronts gnawed through and through, as though the sea were a rodent. The sky offers four separate dramas, the clouds above the ocean are different than the ones over ice that's more than four kilometers thick, puffy cumuli ghost around the islands, while just above us is a blanket of gray. We are sailing through the Avenue of the Ice Giants. Spiky blocks of ice keep watch, their ribbed bodies chiseled out of alabaster. Hammered walls of blue copper and a single albatross, as gentle as a line of chalk, a hundred solitudes away from his nest. That's you, Zeno, plunging at free-fall speed into nothingness, a moment later and you will no longer appear in the drawing.

••• — — •••

Suspected of . . . well what exactly? Where wood is chopped splinters must fall. What made him so furious? Actually there was hardly anything that didn't make him furious. That's not very helpful. I'll give you an example, last year the ship was completely overbooked for this one expedition, the lecturers had to be put up two to a cabin, we were running low on drinking water because people were consuming too much, and for the desalination to kick in the ship has to have a speed of at least fifteen knots, so every night we had to sail to Deception Island and back just to have enough water for breakfast, and that went on several nights in a row, if we'd stayed in the Antarctic one more day we would have run out of fuel. And? That really made him furious. Yes, it's fluttering right here in front me in the train station, the pigeon isn't totally white, you're right, it has a few black spots and two brown stripes, there, on the sides, I have no idea what you call it. We can get original footage from a Columbian TV that had a crew on board, we haven't seen stuff that strong since the incident with the tanker, remember, the one that crashed into the harbor? The workers on the dock saw it heading straight at them, they had fifteen minutes to clear out what they could. Dry fodder, profit is short term, worry is for life, we should rather look at the whole thing from a psychological perspective, student fodder, it's too much to ask people to behave with a mind to a future they won't live to see, hiccup, I'm a pious skeptic, dry cough, I have pills for everything, some make you bigger others make you smaller and some let you forget, and the correct answer is: the thickest book is the book of world records, congratulations, I thank you all, canned meat, I love you all BREAKING NEWS HIJACKED SHIP BOARDED BY SPECIAL FORCES BREAKING NEWS HIJACKED SHIP BOARDED BY SPECIAL FORCES is in large measure suspect

••• —— •••

11.

64°50′3″S, 62°33′1″W

I'M LOOKING DOWN at Neko Harbor (there's still no place I like better), a glacial tongue, an oval bay, and further out a narrow strait hemmed in by jagged, jutting mountains, the humped backs of mighty creatures sleeping away the summer, while kelp gulls fly in lingering spirals. The bay makes the ship seem tiny, insignificant, as if it could be made to disappear using a handheld remote. I breathe in the view until it streams through all my veins and fills my brain. Jeremy is sitting on a stone that's free of snow, pointing his camcorder at the glacier in an effort to capture masses of ice as they crash into the foaming sea. Without warning he points his camera at me, "What a lucky coincidence, here comes the lead actor of the new blockbuster hit *The Penguin Strikes Back*, please share with our television audience exactly when it dawned on you that you would write the history of the Antarctic Cruise Crusade?" In reply I make a disgusted face. The camera doesn't so much as twitch. "And where did you get the idea of using a penguin to play the squeaky wheel?" I shake my head and say nothing. Jeremy jumps up and stamps around me with his heavy boots, bombarding me with further questions while I stare into space so the pushy reporter will go away. "With your permission I'd like to ask one final question, namely who is going to play the role of the penguin, could you at least share that secret with us?" The snow isn't firm enough for rapid movement, our laugher is more nimble than our feet. "Cut. Professor Z., why do you love ice as much as you do?" Jeremy has stopped, his glasses are slightly clouded over.

"Because of its variety."

"Could you explain further?"

"The most beautiful thing on earth: variety."

"Yes of course, we all love variety, but in the ice?"

"There's nothing more varied. A solid body containing gas and liquid."

"Just like human beings. Cut. We are observing a professor on the mound overlooking Neko Harbor, who is attempting to remain serious although he would like to laugh, it is the seriousness of the situation forcing him to do this, for he has recognized how serious the situation really is."

"Go ahead and make fun since everything really is so funny."

"All right then, let's be serious. Cut. Zeno, what would you say is your greatest wish at this moment?"

"I'd like to stay here, Jeremy."

"But you wouldn't be able to survive."

"Who knows, with a tent and a backpack and some dry provisions."

"Well I'm sure the captain would give me a medal or maybe even a raise if I did leave you here, no, wait, it won't work. Paulina would tear my head off."

"I'm tired."

"Already? It's just the start of the season."

"I'm tired of being human."

"You're ok, Mr. Iceberger. Even if you do get off track now and then, still . . ."

"I'm not tired of being me, Jeremy, just tired of being human."

Jeremy takes one step forward, then another, he embraces me, unexpectedly, it's a ritual typically reserved for saying goodbye at the end of the expedition, I give him a firm hug in return, he cries out, but not as a joke, I hear a thudding sound followed by a curse, we separate and watch as the Full HD video camera tumbles down the steep cliff and is stopped by a little ridge in the snow, the thought occurs to me that we could climb down, but then it resumes sliding and picks up speed and vanishes out of sight. We stand there like two boxers who've just learned the fight's been called off, pricking our ears, listening for the sound of the camera hitting the water, but we don't hear a thing. We stare at each other. Although I don't say a single word, the regret must be etched on my face, because Jeremy is quick to console us both: No problem, anyway the interview with you was lousy, the camera is insured and I've shot Neko Harbor before in much better

light. Let's pack up. Jeremy pulls one of the red flags out
of the snow, holds it in his hand like a spear or harpoon,
he must have had the same image in mind.

"Just imagine, what if a whale swallowed the latest
edition of *Daily Turbulences* and then got killed and slit
open and some avid Japanese researchers discover the
camera, what if they take out the memory stick and put it
in a camera that hasn't been corroded by the whale's
stomach juices, and then punch 'play'? What do you
think they'll see? Your face. And what will they hear? 'I'm
tired of being human.' And then they nod and each one
says, me too, and they all decide to climb into the open
belly of the whale, which they staple shut from the inside
before tossing it back into the ocean."

"How will they do that if they're all inside?"

"One of them will have to sacrifice himself, somebody
will have to stay outside and operate the sling lift. Satisfied,
you old pedant you?"

"If that happened I would be overjoyed."

"Let's get a move on, down we come, or how do you say
it in Bavarian?"

"*Obi*, Let's go *obi!*"

Using flag stakes as walking poles we carefully make
our way down, soon we're eye level with the seagulls,
gentoos are scrambling over the craggy outcroppings,
the snow around them is discolored from their urine, the
green color is as pungent as the ammoniac stench. From
the shoreline the glacier looks like a face with a thousand expressions, each posing a different riddle in the
sunlight. It's almost too much, says Jeremy. And I say

nothing. We stand there a while next to each other, hypnotized by all the crevasses into which our thoughts are falling, Father roaming through the house at night, raising his litany to a lament, the louder his voice the deeper he is buried beneath his cry. I have the impression time and again that glaciers are putting on the last act of a bad play.

The ice is here, the ice is there, the ice is all around, before us as a carpet whose knots crack when we step on them, behind us as a mirror broken in a thousand pieces. When the floes graze each other they sound like little bells, when they collide with the hull it echoes like cannon fire. Just four years ago we couldn't make it through at this time of year. On shore Klabautermann goblins compete for our attention with their contortions, while angels guard over us higher up, their wings folded close to their icy bodies. Now and then, when no other being is watching, the Klabautermanns drop into the black water and dive to the bottom to rest. The boundary of the drift ice is so straight it looks like it was drawn with a ruler. For a few minutes I could imagine it thickening and enclosing our ship and not letting go. On the sundeck a barbecue is being set up for an open-air dinner while the ship glides through another strait. The weather is mild, the mood euphoric. The music is already blasting from the speakers, people are expected to dance in their full polar regalia, sunshine, sunshine reggae, a moonboot pas de deux, one couple asks me to take a picture of them, I say, "Say cheese," and she puckers her mouth into a kiss

and says "honeymoon" let the good vibes get a lot stronger,
I won't miss this either.

By the late light of day we cast anchor in a bay full of ice
floes as round as white whales, as narrow as their tailfins
and as sharp as their teeth, a swan is swimming among
them with a bloated head. The sky gradually darkens, a
jaeger rushes out of its nest and pulls a last cry out of the
dusky firmament. I wish there was a letter in the alphabet
for death.

••• — — •••

How did you do it, Carstens, how did you manage to get
our colleague on board the hijacked ship, you're a genius.
If it doesn't help it doesn't hurt, am I some kind of ornithologist, an ordinary pigeon, it tried to land, the floor's
just been mopped, she's slipping and sliding across the
floor, yes that's all, nothing more, well, since you asked
why I was so distracted, the idea of an empty purse causes
people more anxiety than the idea of their own demise.
Would you consider yourself a misanthrope? In a positive
sense of the word. Do you prefer birds to people? Ask my
children. Don't you think that an excessive love of nature
leads to violence, including towards humans? On the
contrary, insufficient love of nature leads to violence, also
towards humans. Are you putting animals and humans on
the same level? They're worth the same aren't they? Aren't
humans a higher being? Not to my knowledge. Let's not
ruin the mood, two deer at the edge of town, the vehicles

come to a stop, the deer trot across the field, the glass is either half empty or overflowing, if you hear the Klabautermann knocking it means he'll stay if you hear him working he'll go away. We have the passenger list, it's amazing how many little VIPs come together when you send a ship to the Antarctic, I want to know everything about every one of them, especially this coal mine king from West Virginia that demolished entire mountainsides before selling his business to Patriot Coal, also about that super-birder who in real life is a porn producer and the news announcer that was fired when he lost his voice, those are the stories we need, Carstens. Of course I don't rummage through the trash, it was the bin for recycled paper, I looked out the window and saw him dumping books, I was curious, I drove over even though it's just around the corner, as if I had sensed what I would find, the nicest things, first editions and autographed copies, they were lying in the bin next to pizza packages and advertising leaflets, I had to save the books, I don't rummage through trash BREAKING NEWS RESCUED PASSENGERS SAFELY HOME BREAKING NEWS RESCUED PASSENGERS SAFELY HOME that came off marvelously

••• — — •••

12.

64°27′1″S, 62°11′5″W

LAST NIGHT, FOR the first time in years, since the hottest summer ever, which followed other hot summers, since the summer when our June climate report was obsolete as early as August, for the first time ever, since the lie I was living daily was operated out of me and my glacier died, there was no looming nightmare. I slept without second sight. When I wake up I feel revived, as though I've undergone a live cell therapy treatment. I lie in bed, a timid light slips under the curtain. One more day, and what a day. Paulina is stretching. Outside our door a passenger goes stomping past on his morning rounds. Paulina's face becomes visible in the light over the nightstand. "Who are you?" I ask. A bewitched maiden, she answers, who has to change into the first creature she sees when she wakes up.

"What a horrible curse!"

"Yes, imagine it could be the head chef. But I'm lucky because I saw you."

"You call that luck? Now you're going to turn into an old man, an ugly old man."

"I'll turn into you, into Zeno. But listen, there's more to it, because you've also been put under a spell, by the same spirit."

"What kind of spirit is that?"

"It's a spirit who's all mixed up, you have to turn into me."

"I'm getting the better deal."

"Then we'll really be together, in our memories as Zeno and Paulina and now as Paulina and Zeno."

She stretches her arm across the gap between the two beds, our fingers interlace, I know of no more binding gesture. I begin massaging her fingers. "Are you afraid of hell?" she asks all of a sudden, while we're still under the covers, turned toward each other. I can't answer right away, I'm focusing on her fingers with the narrowest nails, trying to shake off the thought that this is the last time we'll ever wake up together. With my forefinger I brush her fingertips, one by one, without knowing if her skin will retain these touches. If I were safe inside her fairytale and had one more wish it would be that the river Lethe would flow between the icy continent and Brabant Island.

"Hell is not a place," I finally answer. "It's the sum of all our lapses and failures."

She looks at me confused, her fingers dig into the back of my hand, she presses her thumb so hard into the flesh below my thumb it hurts.

"The realization, much much too late that you didn't do anything when you still could, when you still should have, that is hell. And there's no escape."

"I see," she says, "you're trying to reassure me. She loosens her grip. In your own weird way you're trying to tell me you're not going to hell."

Dan Quentin is standing on a pile of stones, holding a megaphone and directing the red-wrapped extras swarming below him on the ice. Make a mental picture of what the SOS looks like, he blares through the megaphone, in the middle is the circle, the symbol of that which is indestructible, the circle of life, and next to it are two snakes. Why do I say snakes and why do I say there are two? Because there are two basic states, and keep this in mind when you form the S, it's very important, there is the state of contamination and there is the state of purification, there is the poison and there is the cure, are you with me? Dan Quentin puts down his megaphone and surveys his rising work of art: three hundred people awaiting his orders. He appears cheerful, content. In countless interviews he will describe how well it all turned out. And when he's done saying everything he wants to, the announcer will lower her voice and ask how he managed to cope with the drama that came right on the heels of his greatest artistic success. And in a solemn voice Dan Quentin will explain . . . Now, all together, give me an S (red arms reach up high), give me an O (red arms reach up high), give me an S (red arms reach up high) and now, long and loud and proud, give me an S-O-S! (all arms reach up high), it's a funfair, Octoberfest in the southernmost latitudes, voices rise like wisps of smoke, linguistic differences in red, black, white and gray, I'm standing nearby, his face is straining with emotion, the deckhands correct a few bulges in the curves, on this trip the Filipinos take care of everything, even to the point of ironing all angles out of an SOS. The Zodiacs bring further crewmembers ashore, who storm the small rise like straggling soldiers so as not to miss the spectacle.

"That's enough," Quentin calls out to me. "We have enough people already."

"They want to be part of it."

"We don't need them."

"It's too late."

"They should go back, they'll just mess everything up."

"It's too late, the crew also wants to be part of the SOS."

"That wasn't the deal."

"The more the merrier, that's what you said."

"I meant the passengers," Quentin shouts down from his rock pile, then squawks through his megaphone, "Faster, faster." The manager and his adjutants insert the waitresses, cooks, technicians, cabin stewards, launderers into the growing S snake consisting of notaries, executive consultants, general managers and financial analysts, Paulina is there as well, for a second I can make out her face, Ricardo is behind her, he's placed his hands on her shoulders, then I lose sight of her, all of a sudden sunlight floods into our icy party, this is it, Quentin hurries over, tosses me the megaphone, it's now or never, he's ready to seize the moment, a Napoleon of the arts, he rushes to the helicopter with sweeping strides, that's my cue, I radio Jeremy to tell him I'm heading back to the ship, El Albatros has set off to find a breeding site of blue-eyed cormorants that's supposed to be nearby, Beate has found a place in a bend of the second S, the helicopter lifts off, all hands wave, Quentin's manager rushes from one deckhand to the next, probably to remind them to get out of the picture, they are the scaffold that must be dismantled as quickly as possible so that a pure SOS can shine, I ask one of the waiting boatmen to run me back to the *Hansen*, which he is reluctant to do because he doesn't want to miss the spectacle, but his mood improves when I tell him he can go right back, and that he should take everyone still on board, even the receptionist, it's all been arranged with the captain, it's a great day today, a real holiday. The fewer people left on the ship, the easier it will be for me.

From the sundeck I can see the SOS with the naked eye, using binoculars I can make out individual passengers gazing up at the helicopter, which is making a first loop above them, the light flashes in Dan Quentin's lens like an explosion, like a visual start signal. The few personnel who were left behind as an emergency crew are standing at the rail, I tell them to lower one of the life rafts and go aboard and make themselves ready. They buy my story that the captain wishes to practice the maneuver in these waters, with the weather as stable as it is. Now all that's left is for me to convince the stakeholders that they, too, should board the life raft. The drone of the helicopter and the rattling of the crane accompany me into the bowels of the ship.

At last I am alone. On a calm sea and not atop a surge of history, alone on a cruise ship that can be steered with a joystick, as if navigating through the islands of ice were long since nothing but a computer game. Track steering ship control is what this technical miracle is called, one pull of the switch and the ship will follow a preprogrammed route, as Vijay the chief navigator showed me one high-sea day, we were talking about Ladakh and Tibet, storm-free passages make for boring shifts, about Kailash and Gangotri, I entered the open ocean as my destination, the way he showed me, a random point in the wide Atlantic, it seems to be working, the ship is cutting through the water, it will get there without me, too. The bridge has three radar devices (black for sea, yellow for land) and two compasses (one magnetic, one electronic)—I won't need any of it, no more than I need the Automatic Identification System, which shows third parties the position of the MS *Hansen* and lets me know what might be approaching. They will catch up with me. I've taken the flag off the mast and tossed it in the bin marked Plastic Waste.

It's going to be a long day.

Someone will find this notebook, someone will read it and decide to publish it or not. One way or the other, I have no need to explain myself further. One human being is an enigma, a few billion human beings organized in a parasitic system are a catastrophe. Under these circumstances I'm just tired of being human. "It would be lovely to walk the streets with a green knife and scream until I die of the cold." There is an eviscerated bird dangling in front of every human home.

I used to believe I had to fight my insidious misanthropy, today I realize that we have to topple humans off their pedestal in order to save them. What does it matter if a person is blind or deaf, blinkered or benighted? Only big blows are capable of jolting mankind. I am calm and resolute. I pull the master switch, all lights on board go out.

It's high time.

What consoles me? That we will leave nothing behind except fossilized excrement.

When it gets dark I will go out and I will fly, surrounded by thornfish and sea squirts swimming below me, skates and rays gliding away above me. I will fly until my blood has run to ice.

••• ── ── •••

Those are measurements to die for, copper, you can kiss it goodbye, everyone must be called upon to sacrifice, platinum, no one's going to question it, now that's what I call one efficient move, sooner or later our hour will strike, iron, all ravens are black, oil, measurements to die for, we have to be prepared for every contingency, lol, everywhere there are unexplained delays, chromium, we're doing what we can, his epitaph should read: mistrust the survivors, grit your teeth and get on with it, whoever blinks has lost by half, gold, shit happens, no one's going to question it except for those who deny it, you can't do anything about it, of course I want to get home as soon as possible, no, I'm not just standing here looking at pigeons on purpose, what do I know, the way she's scowling, it's upsetting, it's really upsetting, coal, it was programmed wrong, we got off with a black eye, uranium. We searched the ship, there's no one on board, we're certain that there's no one on board, no idea what happened to the hijacker, we found something, some sign of life, next to the steering console on the bridge, a notebook, it's full of writing, in German if I'm not mistaken, it might help us understand what he did. We fled to the south, where dollars drop from the sky like snowflakes, the business climate and the apparent temperature is trending toward bankruptcy. I was wrong, there's still someone on board, we discovered her on the monitors, an older woman, she was wandering up and down the passageways, she seems dazed, her eyes are glassed over, she says she was attacked by a penguin, not very believable, she claims not to know anything about the hijacking, I know, she says she was sound asleep because of the powerful antibiotics, we'll have to question her of course. The overweight will have to weigh things over, morning, evening, and in the fall, prepared for everything, we're infesting now in our future, the revolution will not be televised, be prepared for everything, the revolution will not be televised, BREAKING NEWS LIGHTS GO OUT TONIGHT FOR FIVE MINUTES BREAKING NEWS LIGHTS GO OUT TONIGHT FOR FIVE MINUTES on and on without end

••• — — — •••

Acknowledgments

Thanks to all who generously shared their expertise and who helped me, on land as well as at sea:

Dr. Reinhard Böhm for the lively glacier tutorial
Kristina Dörlitz for the excellent research assistance
Alexandra Föderl-Schmid for the second commission
Petra Glardon for the wonderful iceberg photos
Prof. Dr. Wilfried Haeberli for his edifying
  encouragement
Christoph Hofbauer for his high-powered advice
Mijnheer Hans Huyssen for the music
Angelika Klammer for her inspired and inspiring editing
Freddy Langer for the friendly press service
Dr. Rudi Mair for the conversation about Alpine climate
  and Antarctic overwintering
Borrego Pedro Rosa Mendes for the days and nights at
  the Tejo

Compañero José F. A. Oliver for his empathetic reading
   of the manuscript
Papa Heinz Renk for showing me the Tyrolean glaciers
Dr. Miguel Rubio-Godoy for the avalanche of calamities
Dr. Christine Scholten for the medical review
Dorothée Stöbener for the first commission
Susann Urban for the gift of the title
Juli Zeh for the wielding the red pen

Hurtigruten Shipping for their double hospitality

The poems cited in the text are by Samuel Taylor
   Coleridge, Klabund and Pablo Neruda

On the Typeface

This book is set in Electra, a typeface designed by William Addison Dwiggins for use on Linotype typesetting machines in 1935. Dwiggins, a mildly eccentric book designer, illustrator, calligrapher and creator of marionettes, is credited with coining the term "graphic design". Dwiggins's foray into type design began with a challenge from the Mergenthaler Linotype Company, after he had criticized the dearth of usable san serifs. Electra was Dwiggins's first type design for book setting and would be one of his most enduring.

While the popular book faces of his time were revivals of fifteenth- and sixteenth-century printing types, Dwiggins sought to create a typeface that reflected the modern environment. As his friend and fellow illustrator Rudolph Ruzicka commented, Electra was "the crystallization of [Dwiggins's] own calligraphic hand." Its unbracketed serifs, flat arches, and open counters make for a face mild in pretence but alive in personality. Dwiggins explained, "The weighted top serifs of the straight letters of the lower case: that is a thing that occurs when you are making formal letters with a pen, writing quickly. And the flat way the curves get away from the straight stems: that is a speed product."